THE SCHUBE
SONG CYCLES

THE SCHUBERT SONG CYCLES

with thoughts on performance

BY

GERALD MOORE

HAMISH HAMILTON
LONDON

First published in Great Britain 1975
by Hamish Hamilton Ltd
90 Great Russell Street London WC1

Copyright © Gerald Moore 1975

SBN 241 89082 9

Filmset and printed by BAS Printers Limited, Wallop, Hampshire

ACKNOWLEDGEMENTS

I am indebted to Gerald Duckworth & Co. Ltd for the numerous quotations I have made from Richard Capell's *Schubert's Songs*.

I have quoted from the following and I am grateful for the publishers' permission: *Selected Lyrics of Heine* by Humbert Wolfe (The Bodley Head Ltd): *Music and Musicians* by Martin Cooper (Messrs Hutchinson & Co. Ltd): and Eric Blom in *Grove's Dictionary of Music and Musicians* (Macmillan, London and Basingstoke, the Macmillan Company of Canada and St. Martin's Press, New York).

CONTENTS

PREFACE

This book was written under compulsion, the compulsion of my love for Franz Peter Schubert. I cannot leave him alone and find myself in the evening of my life turning more and more to the master whom Artur Schnabel described as the composer nearest to God. No one ever expressed himself with such utter lack of artificiality; so spontaneous is his song that the process of transplantation from mind to manuscript without loss of freshness or bloom is miraculous. His heart was full of music which in its unerring directness, unsurprising naturalness and sublime eloquence uplifts the soul. The drudgery of sitting before a blank page, waiting for inspiration, forcing ideas into shapely proportions was unknown to him for the ideas blossomed and sprouted like the springing herb beside the banks of his beloved brook.

We are delighted again and again by this or that composer's melodies, but melody with Schubert assumed a meaning unprecedented in depth and subtlety. Whether sad or gay, quiescent or animated it flows with inexhaustible freshness, burgeoning with rhythmical impulse and mobility, and alive with inventive turns of direction which, at first surprising seem with hindsight inevitable. A Schubertian melody is a composition in itself with a freedom and variety of colour inspired by— and felicitously reflecting—'the tune of the words'.

Who could be more spontaneous than the young miller in *Der Neugierige* when, after asking the eternal question 'Does she love me?' complains that 'the flowers and stars cannot tell me?'

sie kön - nen mir al - le nicht sa - gen,

The very pitch of the little passage with its fitful step up and then down expresses uncertainty. But behold the confidence that comes with the resolve to seek an answer from his companion brook

mein Bäch-lein will ich fra - gen,

Here is a superb sweep, a glow that, try as he will, the singer could not possibly bestow on the first pallid complaint.

How has this been achieved? Let us take the *melisma* away and we get

mein Bäch-lein will ich fra - gen,

Radiance is missing. The *melisma** is the thing!

This stringing of notes to one syllable is a device as ancient as music itself but one wonders whether, in the nineteenth century its elaborate embroidery had any bearing on a situation or was there merely to demonstrate vocal virtuosity. No such doubts arise with Schubert for his *melisma* is purposeful, giving meaning to the word and colour to the mood. It is a proposition wholly dependent on the singer's handling of these *melismata*: the intrusive 'H' or the vulgar slide (as distinct from the controlled *legato* and discriminating *portamento*) have no part in it.

Singer and accompanist will see in the following pages that I try to deal with problems as they arise such as the distinction between *sf* (or *fp*) and the sign > which we call an accent; and since the latter occurs more frequently in these songs than any other sign it is as well to understand how we propose to treat it. In Schubert this mark does not invariably call for an increase of tone or sudden stab: here is evidence that it was not intended to be a routine accent.

This chord comes in the third bar of *Gute Nacht* the opening song of *Winterreise*. Surely the *fp* was sufficient unto itself while the 'accent' sign if regarded in the accepted sense is redundant—or has it some other implication here? I believe so, I think it calls for a slight prolongation on that chord, ever so slight so as not to distort the shape of the passage: it is performed with such sensitivity that the operation becomes hardly perceptible. I call it a time stress. It occurs and should be interpreted often in this way. Undeniably it sometimes calls for an accent in the accepted sense but with a force decidedly less than a *sforzando*. We learn to read between the lines, to employ a little imagination so that in *Ständchen* when we find

*Two or more notes sung to one syllable.

we see that extra pressure of tone on 'ach' has meaning where it would be without reason on 'durch'. Let 'durch'—while still preserving its *mezzo voce* quality—be given a little more time, a little lyrical freedom.

Now the reader, after my suggested 'time stress' or 'prolongation' will begin to wonder if I am an advocate of *rubato*. I confirm his suspicions by saying that I am. In my opening paragraph I made a rod for my own back by declaring I could not leave Schubert alone, a statement that invites the retort 'Why couldn't you?'

Let me defend myself.

I have performed these songs with many singers some hundreds of times over the last half century and while I was sometimes criticized on one count or another, I was never condemned for my love of elasticity or flexibility; nor did I ever find myself at odds with my partner. The bar line is not made of iron and the singer should not be imprisoned by it. Because of the over-riding importance of the phrase, one bar (or measure) can take more time than another, perhaps because it holds the high point in this phrase, a high point (not necessarily the topmost note) by reason of a subtle turn in the melody or because of a vital word or poignant change of harmony in the accompaniment and it can be delivered gently and persuasively or driven home with force as the occasion requires.

The literal translation of *rubato* is 'robbed', not 'borrowed' and it is a fallacy to believe the stolen time should be repaid, that after the slowing up, compensation is made by hastening. Never returning what he takes, the robber has one desire in common with the musician and his *rubato*, namely the avoidance of detection.

Rhythm means something infinitely more than a mechanical counting of beats, bars, obedience to the metronome and, as can be seen in the little excerpt from *Ständchen*, the spirit of the word sometimes influences the shape of the melodic line and this line, provided it is not offensive to musicianly good taste and to the shapeliness of form, is supple and free.

In my interpretation of these songs I have treated the performers as a pair and I shall be disappointed if the singer feels I have given too much attention to the pianoforte. For long it has been my aim to promote the accompanist but there is no doubt in my mind, that the heavier burden of responsibility falls on the singer; it is he who *presents* the song, who marries the word with the music and by his countenance reflects without hyperbole the mood of the song: he does not look lugubrious in *Ungeduld* or bland in *Der Jäger*. The listeners' eyes are on him, their ears, however, are opened impartially to voice and pianoforte.

This is indeed a partnership, for the singer knows every note and appreciates every nuance of the accompaniments; their technical difficulties he does not need to worry about unless he asks for the impossible.

On his side the pianist may be ignorant of vocal problems but he knows the melodic line intimately, is able to anticipate its every nuance and curve; more, he has studied the text—he needs to, for more often than not his introduction will be expected to evoke a mood (*Feierabend: Die liebe Farbe*) or set the scene (*Der Lindenbaum: Die Stadt*) before the singer has opened his mouth; and frequently his postlude will bear the burden when his partner has said his all. Urgent expression, moreover, is not to be reserved for these moments only with the pianist resting on his oars during the course of the song. The pianoforte must sing. Even in slow moving songs, nay, especially in slow moving songs (*Das Wirtshaus: Ihr Bild*) the accompanist is very much alive. He on whose banner is inscribed 'self-effacement' is no inspiration to anyone. It may help him to shed the shackling cloak of timidity he has worn and been persuaded to wear if he recalls that all the illustrious composers of Lied, mélodie or song—poles apart in individual style—are alike in one respect, they are all pianists.

Of that great line of composers, none other than the founder Franz Peter Schubert would have touched these *Müllerin* verses which, with their singing stream would have been anathema to Schumann, Wolf and Brahms. On the periphery Loewe would have found their lack of sensationalism an unsurmountable handicap: Grieg, perhaps, with his square tunes and flat rhythms would have made another 'Haugtussa Cycle' with some troll or water sprite. But Schubert with his unspoiled nature took the poems to his heart, accepted them at their face value: he believed that the brook gave comfort to the poor lad, so that hearing the words

'Und wenn sich die Liebe dem Schmerzen entringt,

Ein Sternlein, ein neues, am Himmel erblinkt'.

made sublime on the wings of Schubert, we too believe and are not ashamed if our eyes are wet.

Here was a giant (how he would have recoiled from this epithet!) who had marched with the mighty Goethe in over seventy poems of drama, depth and grandeur—*Prometheus, Ganymed, Erlkönig,* the Wilhelm Meister songs—and yet was able to transport himself back to the age of innocence.

Schubert's *Gretchen am Spinnrade, Erlkönig* and other masterpieces all bear the unmistakable stamp of genius, they were written in his teens when naturally enough not all his works attained this supernal level. Had he set the twenty *Maid of the Mill* songs at this time, the cycle as a whole would have been less wonderful than it is, but by a benign act of providence the Müller lyrics did not come his way until he had reached the height of his powers. He was twenty-five years old with three quarters of his life's spell behind him when he began *Das Wandern.*

The cycle is a story of springtime and summer, of a sensitive lad's love and of a maiden's fickleness; through it all runs a thread—the mill-stream, the 'liebes Bächlein', which proves to be the one constant companion to the lover and to whose cool depths he finally commits himself and is gently rocked to oblivion.

Unlike the miller, whose songs run the gamut from exultation to despair, the winter wanderer is without hope; sometimes a dream brings easement, or indulgence in self-deception induces temporary forgetfulness, but never does he know a moment of gladness.

It is one of the marvels of this cycle that Schubert was able to create such extraordinary variety of expression within so restricted an emotional range.

In *Die Schöne Müllerin* the lad shares the stage with his stream; we meet the girl, see the master miller, we know and learn to hate the hunter in his green jacket who steals the girl's fancy. But in *Die Winterreise* we meet no one—no human being until the very last song. Though aware of the unwelcome attention of the crows, in *Im Dorfe* of the snarling dogs—(even the charcoal burner who gives the wanderer a night's rest is unseen)—it is only with the appearance of the organ grinder that some vestige of human understanding is manifested: he is seen from afar 'Drüben hintern Dorfe' yet we know him and esteem him for it is his frail hand that steadies the demented man.

In some of the songs where the wayfarer is on the move there is, quite apart from the obvious 2/4 walking stride, a similar rhythmical pattern. It is so recondite that one cannot help wondering whether the composer employed it consciously or not: too slight to be a leitmotif it is only made obvious on rare occasions, in fact I had studied the cycle for years before I discovered it.

The above comes eight times in the accompaniment to *Gute Nacht* and is barely to be noticed, but in *Auf dem Flusse* it is the singer's theme and is very much to the fore,

and is heard fourteen times. A hint of it can be discerned in the accompaniment to *Rückblick* (the introduction, bars 1, 3, 5) and in the vocal line of *Irrlicht* ('Bin gewohnt das Irregehen' bars 17, 18) again in the climax (31, 32) of *Die Krähe*. Most strongly is it in evidence in *Der Wegweiser* where it appears eight times in the pianoforte or voice part.

The little figure is hardly an umbilical cord but it admits of relationship between those particular songs.

No song in either cycle ought to be assessed on its individual merit for each is a vital member of a majestic and immortal structure, a structure greater than the sum of its parts.

Schwanengesang is only referred to as a cycle for convenience's sake, being so named by the publisher who issued all fourteen songs simultaneously after the composer's death. While there is no thread running through them, four of the Heine and most of the Rellstab verses have 'sehnsucht' as their theme and this includes the delicious *Taubenpost* of Seidl, added as Schubert's own swan song.

It was unfair to Rellstab to couple his name in this collection with Heine and yet there are four songs which gladden the heart of every Schubertian—the charming *Liebesbotschaft* and *Abschied*, the raging *Aufenthalt* and of course *Ständchen* with its tender transports and a beauty which we are apt to overlook because of its popularity and consequent mutilation. The remaining three poems are unremarkable and long-winded.

In the last August of his life Schubert set six Heinrich Heine poems, every one of them a paradigm of song writing. Here was the Master with death only three months away treading new ground yet seemingly knowing every inch of the way, every unnecessary trimming being cut away and only the essence remaining—only the truth, sometimes sublime, sometimes unbearable, but always soul-stirring in its revelation.

The three cycles were eloquently summed up by Martin Cooper with these words 'In these final products of his extraordinary genius Schubert carried the German Lied to heights of grandeur and depths of feeling never equalled by his successors in the field'.

I apologize for the constant use of the terms *forte*, *piano*, *rallentando*, *accelerando* and the like, but I decided that any attempt to find variants for them led to confusion. This was discovered by the conductor at rehearsal who time after time stopped the orchestra at the same passage with the cry 'No, no, no, it must be the beating of the heart'. 'What does he mean?' asked one exasperated player of another—'He means *pianissimo*' was the reply.

My friend Sir Neville Cardus for twenty years wrote 8000 words every week for the *Manchester Guardian* on the subject of cricket (a cabbalistic rite peculiar to England, performed in the open air during the summer months when it is not raining). 'It is possible' Sir Neville confesses 'that towards the end of the season I was apt to repeat myself'.

I am very much afraid that I shall be accused of repetitiveness except by the most generous of readers.

In conclusion a word concerning my dedicatees.

I have long regarded Richard Capell as one of the foremost authorities on the Lieder of Schubert; his book *Schubert's Songs* is without parallel and should adorn the library of every lover of music for it is written with intimate understanding, passion, and vividness of colour. I have learned much from it and, thanks to the courtesy of the publishers (Gerald Duckworth & Co. Ltd.) have quoted from it with some freedom.

In the world of music Dietrich Fischer-Dieskau is pre-eminent among singers with a genius that is expressed in Lieder, opera and more recently in conducting. One of the joys of my life was my partnership with this man; working with him was an inspiration and I am aware that in his company I went deeper than ever before into the heart of these great cycles. So much in Schubert's art 'reposes in an understanding between friends ' (Capell): there is everything to be said for rehearsing, for advanced planning but in the final reckoning the presentation or expression must bear no evidence of being thought out, and this is where Fischer-Dieskau is unique for he sings with the freshness, freedom and rapture of new-born experience.

He is the supreme Schubert singer of our time.

DIE SCHÖNE MÜLLERIN

I. DAS WANDERN

IN THE very first song, *Das Wandern*, the performers find a problem
which recurs often during the course of the cycle: namely, how to treat
the strophic song. The two pages of music, twenty bars in all, are
repeated five times, and with disarming economy Schubert—apart
from the instruction *Mässig geschwind* (moderately quick) has only given
us a few recommendations. It would seem that the order of expression
marks relating to the first verse *piano, mezzopiano, pianissimo* etc.
should similarly be applied to the four other verses whether their
subject be rippling water or heavy millstone, surely a proposition
without reason rendering the music meaningless. If Schubert wanted
each verse to be treated with the colour, weight, and flow that the words
suggest why did he not insert expression marks for each verse? The
simple answer is that he did not have time. Schubert undoubtedly
credited singer and pianist with imagination and I outline my ideas how
this should be exercised. As in all songs under review, the suggestions I
make are not dogmatic but are offered to stimulate the vision of the two
performers.

To begin with then, the fourth bar of the Introduction has a *fermata*
but under it in the Mandyczewski Edition which I take as authentic is
the significant word *Fine*.

Ex. 1

This *Fine* obviously applies only to the very end of the song (the
postlude seen in many editions—bars 21 to 24—does not appear in
Mandyczewaki where the repeat is made from bar 20) and so in my
opinion should the *fermata*. Why bring the movement to a sudden
standstill? It would be equally illogical to make a pause on the last

chord of the introduction to *Mein* (Song No. XI). Therefore, for the
first four verses, this bar is played *a tempo*, and the singer makes his
entry with an eager promptitude. He remembers to keep in character;
it is a young lusty countryman who is singing and a healthy *forte* should
be maintained throughout until he comes to bars 17–20.

Ex. 2

das Wan - dern, das   Wan - dern, das   Wan - dern, das   Wan - dern.

The fond echo of the last two bars should be observed but the
accents—must they be stressed? Decidedly they should be; not with
sudden dynamic bursts of tone but by allowing them a little more time.
Schubert was not afraid to write *sforzando* as we shall see in *Halt*,
Am Feierabend, *Ungeduld*, etc., etc., but he would have been unusually
dramatic in a *pianissimo* phrase but two bars duration had he asked
for *sforzandi* on the first beat of each bar. The stresses, I repeat, are
allowed a fraction more time, hardly to be noticed by the listener, and
leaving the flow undisturbed. A glance at *Trockne Blumen* (song XVIII)
bears out my contention that Schubert used the sign > for a rhythmical
purpose and a *fp* for a dynamic surge

Ex. 3

in bars 30 and 35 respectively.

In verse two the light airy quality the singer aims to use in *Wohin*
(song II) should be anticipated. 'Von Wasser haben wir's gelernt',
suggests the clear silvery stream and needs *legato* singing, very much the
reverse from the vigorous and impulsive 'Das Wandern ist des Müllers
Lust', and the piano murmurs in a quiet rippling, as far as is possible
for it to do so in this sonorous section of the instrument.

For the turning mill-wheels churning the water, more excitement is
needed and a step up in volume compared to verse two. The pianist can
help materially by using a *staccato* touch especially in his two little
interludes in bars 7, 8, and 11, 12,

Ex. 4

where the pedal helps to give a splashing effect.

But it is to the fourth verse 'The mill stones, how heavy they are' that the singer obviously gives most weight. His line is *non-legato* and robust and the pianist's octaves in bars 13–16 are ponderous; these bars are *fortissimo*.

A word of warning to the singer.

In all the semiquaver passages let there be no intrusive aspirate;

Ex. 5

critical self-listening must be exercised. Any Tom, Dick or Harry can trample through these phrases with the help of this insufferable H, and the accompanist should not hesitate to tell his partner if he hears it.

Through all the features so far described to us, the stream, the mill with its wheel and stones, runs the strong vein of resolution, but now in the last verse, impetuosity lessens to be replaced by a more reflective mood. The singer warns us of this change by adopting a slightly slower tempo, and we are made aware of his longing by the deliberation and earnestness he puts into his last four bars 'Und Wandern, und Wandern'.

My aversion to the *fermata* in the interludes does not hold good before verse 5: here the pianist not only makes a *diminuendo* but helps the singer by pausing slightly on the last chord in anticipation of the quieter nature of the verse.

II. WOHIN

WHEREAS IN the first song excited anticipation seized the journeyman miller, it is in *Wohin* and *Halt* (songs II and III) that it is realized.

These are the two songs in the cycle where innocent happiness reaches its peak. To be sure there are joyous transports to come in *Ungeduld* and *Mein* but by the time we reach these songs the lad is deeply in love and whether or not one can be wholly carefree after giving one's heart to another depends on the man himself. I do not think the young miller could. We see this in *Danksagung an den Bach* where the boy realizes his heart is captivated by the maiden, a song undoubtedly contented and peaceful, but not untinged with a gentle melancholy, an uncertainty as to what the future holds in store.

Wohin is all sunshine. To the rippling accompaniment—in which the *pianissimo* right hand takes precedence over the left hand—the singer gives us a simple blissful melody. But it is not so simple as it looks. We do not want to anatomise the lovely thing to make each phrase clinically precise at the expense of the whole, for it must be sung as if it were the easiest and most natural tune in the world, but without robbing the singing of spontaneity some thought should be expended on the phrasing. What for instance, is the high point in bars 3 and 4?

Ex.1

Ich hört' ein Bäch-lein rau - schen wohl aus dem Fel-sen-quell,

It is the first syllable of 'rauschen', and this is stressed by making the four preceding quavers leading notes; notes that press on to this high point. 'Rauschen' is emphasized not by more tone but by energetic enunciation. It has to be practised because neither the over-all *legato* line nor the accompaniment must be disturbed. This phrase is echoed with slight variation often and so are the onomatopoeic 'Rauschen' and

Ex.2

Ich weiß nicht, wie mir wur - de, nicht, wer den Rat mir
gab, ich muß-te auch hin-un - ter mit mei-nem Wan-der-stab,

A subtle difference is made between the smiling perplexity of 'I know not what came over me nor who advised me'—sung with especial lightness—and the decided 'I had to follow'—where more tone is allowed.

In Mandyczewski the first beats of 11 and 12 have *appoggiaturas*—but they are treated as indicated above.

After the *pp* 'und immer heller rauschte und immer heller der Bach' the composer wants a *crescendo* and the words are repeated as if we were drawn to the very edge of the water and can hear it gushing: then to a *subito pp* the question is asked 'Ist das denn meine Strasse?'

Ex. 3

It is the miller's first meeting with his stream, the stream which will be his constant companion through all the joys and sorrows that lie ahead. The question, all innocent wonderment, is deliciously conveyed by changes of key to A minor and B major.

As if in acknowledgement that the joyous gurgle of the water has bewitched him

Ex. 4

the pianoforte bass joins the vocal line in full accord.

Schubert, knowing our enthusiasm will have caused us to louden a little, gives a *pp* sign at the 'Es singen wohl die Nixen', and it is good to observe this for it gives an impression of incredulity as much as to say 'It cannot be'. But it *can* be, for the confirmation comes with the repetition of the words and calls for more tone again.

Most loving care is needed for the following

Ex. 5

es   gehn ja Müh - len - rä - der_ in__ je - dem kla - ren Bach.

This wants a beautiful *legato* line giving no extra emphasis to the highest notes.

I hope it will be remarked that, though there are dynamic rises and falls in the vocal line, not once have I suggested the tone should rise to a *forte*. Everything is contained in a narrow compass and never, even in the most excited moments, should the level be more than a *mezzo forte*.

For Schubert to ask for a *rallentando* at the close of a song is almost unheard of, but this is not to say he held a routine objection to it. In *Wohin* however a conventional slowing down would spoil the picture for the little stream flows on as blithely as ever. From 74 where the *diminuendo* begins the pianist plays with ever lessening tone and arrives on his final *pp* chord without hesitation and holds it: the stream does not slow down.

III. HALT

'I SEE a mill peeping through the trees, and hear the splash of its wheels. It seems to sing a sweet welcome to me so inviting is the house with its windows gleaming in the bright sunshine. Dear little brook was this your meaning?'

After the *pianissimo* close of *Wohin* we are startled by the sudden *forte* on the first note of the introduction. It is full of excitement for the first twenty bars as the miller lad catches his first glimpse of the mill.

How meticulously Schubert has indicated his wishes through this

rousing affair—the immediate decrease of tone after the *forte*, a still further decreasing after *piano* (all contained, be it noted, in the span of a single bar) to be followed by that assertive F sharp in the bass (2) whose accent here, coming within the framework of *piano* needs time to allow it due significance, then the unhurried bouncing *staccato* in the left hand. This pattern, bars 1 to 4, is repeated in the dominant minor 5 to 8 before the energetic aggressive octaves of 9, 10. So much enthusiasm—so much vitality! If he plays this introduction as Schubert has marked, the pianist is doing well; much more, his partner will be invigorated.

The singer's entry is impetuous, so impatient is he, he can hardly wait for the turning mill wheel figure in the bass to be rounded off before he attacks and is aiming for the word 'Mühle'. (The semiquaver arch alluded to as the mill wheel figure is a recurring feature of the song.)

Above the running accompaniment the vocal line is declamatory and the singer needs a bracing *forte*, he does not seek the smooth line he needed in *Wohin*. 'Durch Rauschen' (16) is even more excited than bar twelve.

There is a rhythmic interplay between voice and pianoforte in bars 18, 19 and 20, 21

and it is fascinating when the partners in complete accord give wings to the first half of these bars but treat the quavers with a tight rein.

From this point (21) for fourteen bars, and without loss of ardour, the fervour becomes less ebullient, in fact, yes, sentimental; and none the worse for that as the young man describes the welcoming appearance of the house and the good cheer its bright windows seem to exude.

A decided reduction in tone and a true *legato* line make this change of mood apparent. I have put slurs on the second half of 23 and 24, for the faintest *portamento* on these rather melting bars seems natural, an out-pouring of one who longs for a warm welcome. The pianist prepares the way by calm playing of bar 22 and he must relish his unison with the voice in 25 and 29.

Resumption of vigour, as in the opening section, comes at 38 'und die Sonne, wie helle von Himmel sie scheint' (and the sun how brightly it shines in the heavens) but, when the lad asks of his guide the stream

'Is this what you meant?' the *subito piano* brings an intimate feeling into the music.

To the words 'War es also gemeint' there is a dissonance in the pianoforte which almost sounds a note of warning as the song dies away; it is but faintly heard however and fails to cast a cloud over the prevailing optimism.

The semiquavers flowing in the pianoforte treble must always be heard, yet they are subservient—especially in the energetic section—to the bass.

IV. DANKSAGUNG AN DEN BACH

'Is THIS what you meant?' (the closing words of *Halt*) are at once repeated here, so we make only the shortest pause between the two songs.

The lad has fallen under the spell of the master's daughter and this song expresses a tender acknowledgement to the stream for leading him to her.

After the Introduction the singer glides in without effort, without warning us that he has taken a deep breath: he gives us a steady *legato* flow of sound, nearly always *pp* or *p*. Singer and pianist listen carefully each to the other, for the vocal line and the upper voice in the pianoforte blend in a heart-warming duet.

Ex.1

War es al - so ge-meint, mein rau - schen-der Freund? dein

Sin-gen, dein Klin-gen,   war es al - so ge-meint, war es al - so ge-meint?

To communicate this with conviction it is not enough for the singer to
rely on his 'flair'. Feeling and temperament may be there but these
endowments are insufficient in themselves to make these phrases truly
expressive. We look for the high points, high points which are prompted
by the words, or by the line, or by the underlying harmony in the
pianoforte, or by a combination of all these.

Elasticity and freedom—governed by good taste—are most acceptable but they are found only after search and experiment. To begin
with the singer at all costs avoids an automatic accent on the first
beat of each and every bar, a slavish adherence to this lazy habit merely
because 'it is the down beat' will rob the music of its even serenity. As
if to refute my argument, it so happens that in Ex. 1. the first beats of
7 and 9 do get a time stress on them, but 5 is as smooth as maybe; the
semiquavers 'rauschender' in 6 are as important as 'Freund' and are by
no means glossed over; the notes in bar 8 have the same volume as the
top G in 9: a *crescendo* here gives an impression of effort.

These opening phrases of the singer are all *pp*; within this restricted
range the first stress comes on bar 7 'Your singing and your rippling',
not because we reach the highest note in the group here, but because of
the significance of the words. On the contrary in 8 and 9 it is not the
words that demand emphasis, 'war es also gemeint' (they have been
heard six times within half a minute), it is the melodic line; the two
semiquaver F sharps therefore should be leisurely.

Care should be taken by the singer to avoid brandishing his high
notes—merely because they are high notes.

Ex.2

Zur Mül-le-rin hin! so lau-tet der Sinn.

The high G in 11, the F natural in 12 are almost parenthetical.

It is only by trial and error that the young performer will find out
these secrets for himself. They are secrets indeed, for the singing of this
song—as in *Wohin*—must sound natural with unaffected flow.

Ex.3

zur Mül-le-rin hin, zur Mül-le-rin hin!

Schubert wants more tone (*mf*) at the verse's end 'Zur Müllerin hin'—'To the maid of the mill'—the words and the vocal line call for it, bar 17 every bit as enthusiastic as 16.

The minor mode ('Did she send you?'—'Have you bewitched me?') lasts only a few bars (22–24) until the major 'I have found what I sought' where all becomes more subdued than in verse 1. But bar 33 'I looked for work for hands and heart' more animation not in pace but in spirit is needed and the final bars 'I have enough and to spare' (marked *mf*) are sung with a full and generous heart, plenty of time being allowed on the first syllable of 'genug'.

Ex. 4

voll-auf ge-nug, voll-auf ge-nug!

A word, allow me, for the Prologue, repeated note for note between the verses and again in the Postlude.

Ex. 5

It is unnecessary to strain the reader's patience by saying how smoothly this must be played. No note or notes should self-conciously obtrude in this passage and most certainly no conventional *crescendo* on the arch in bar 2.

The grace notes if played without due care and attention can give the impression of a triumphant flourish: any pianist guilty of this rude offence would be well advised to seek some other occupation, these notes are played slowly and softly, with no accent on arrival on the second beat of the bar—no accents whatsoever.

And yet, and yet, there are certain notes in this four bar passage that need consideration. These are penultimate or leading notes which, played unhurriedly, given their full value, contribute tellingly to the eloquence of the passage. Let the pianist *think* about these notes as he plays. They are marked on the above Example with an X.

V. AM FEIERABEND

WE HAVE seen how the stream in the last three songs responds to the mood of the journeyman miller with its light-hearted rippling, its excitement, its gentle motion. Now the water gushes with a fiercer energy.

'O that I had a thousand arms that I could turn these clamorous wheels, could lift the grind stones! O that I could attract the attention of the maiden, that she might see my good will!'

The frustration, repressed passion are reflected in the Introduction.

The longest beats in those four bars are the rests, especially in bars two and four. But do I really propose that the rests, where nothing is happening, should be stretched? Yes, slightly, for these silences throw the violence of the chords into greater relief. No sustaining pedal is to be used until the semiquavers in bars 4, 5, and 6 which are tossed off with brilliance.

Thoroughly out of countenance with himself the miller's outburst is declamatory and harsh and the metronome tempo should be between 88 or 96 to the dotted crotchet.

The thought of the maiden 'that she might see my good will' at bar 16, brings a sudden change of temper, it is now in the major and is sung with more *legato* and a tenderness almost reminiscent of 'ei, willkommen' in 'Halt' with its suggestion of *sehnsucht*.

Ex.2

But vitality sinks to a low ebb at the words 'Why is my arm so weak? Any apprentice could do as well as I'.

Ex.3

As the fury of the opening yields to longing (Ex. 2) and now to weakness, so the pace slows down. Breathless fatigue does not call for a sustained vocal line, so the singer makes his meaning more credible if he breathes whenever it is possible for him to do so. At a quick *tempo* this is difficult and is helped by the pianoforte if the second chord of each pair is less in tone than the first, as if the excited lad were panting from exhaustion.

'And now I sit in the evening hour with the other mill-hands in the presence of the Master and his daughter.'

Ex.4

After all the animation, bar 36 comes on us so suddenly that the pianist has but two bars in which to make preparation for the singer's entry. Only a slower tempo (♩. = 66 or 72) and the unruffled distinctness of the alto figure in his right hand will effect this. Now all is cool and comfortable. The singer will be helped by these two bars and on his entry may hold back the tempo even more if he has a mind to.

At bars 44, 45 the master enters the room introduced by the piano—one can imagine him seating himself with a grunt of satisfaction at 45, with chords that should be played squarely (*mf*). We are not in a lady's drawing room but in the parlour of an unpolished countryman.

Ex. 5

As the master speaks of his satisfaction with the day's work we keep to no tempo: it is recitative ruled by no metronomic beat. Sung *molto legato* with a heavy deliberation we hear the voice of authority commanding the respectful attention of the mill-hands. The whole section 36 to 51 is performed in a matter-of-fact way with a snug appreciation of creature comfort, yet the singer remembers that he is simulating the master and a darkening of colour will make his utterance more plausible.

'Und das liebe Mädchen sagt allen eine Gute Nacht' ('and the dear girl says goodnight to us all') demands a tender tone from the singer expressive of his longing, and he sees to make this contrast a telling one, how important it was that the preceding bars should be sonorous, for now it is evident, though expressed so softly, that the lad's heart is captured (52–55). Ah, but the realization that she does not so much as glance in his direction stabs him to the soul (the *sfortzando* chord in 56).

Ex. 6

The accompanist's *forte* (59) covers the singer's 'Nacht' intentionally and it would be wrong for the pianist to lessen his tone politely, equally wrong too for the singer to make a *subito forte*. The lad's mind is confused and this imbalance matches it.

'O that I had a thousand arms' etc. is repeated, but this time with greater heat, the accompaniment bass figure

here sparks off even more agitation than the earlier

heard in the first verse. Nowhere is the unsettled state of the boy more vividly in evidence than in the closing bars, with its violent *forte* and its sudden *piano*.

Ex.7

Bars 83–85 are sung with the knowledge that the girl is out of reach: no response to the lad's admiration for her has been shown. The pianist's first four quavers (86) should be shaped as 'treuen Sinn' was shaped, for the singer slowed down these notes to give expression to his longing. Thereafter the descending passage moves forward to the *tempo* of 82 always getting softer as the maid disappears from view. The last two chords are quick, short and brittle.

This song is a Kaleidoscope with its changing pace, colour and mood.

VI. DER NEUGIERIGE

THIS EXQUISITE song murmured with simplicity and sincerity makes formidable demands on the singer, needing as it does a smooth line, a beautiful tone and refined musicianship. The listener is not made aware of any such problems for the song is nearly always gentle as the miller stands musing by the stream.

'I question neither flower nor star, they cannot tell me what I wish to know for I am no gardener and the stars are too distant'.

Even without the words to guide us, the melodic line alone suggests a question.

Ex.1

It is a common fault to skimp the second syllable of 'frage' and 'keine'; in bars 5 and 7 these semiquavers should be given more than their full value. All through the first 20 bars the rests should be apparent for these silences after each phrase contribute to the miller's uncertainty. All *pianissimo*: only on bar 11 we want more heart, more warmth.

Was ever a question mark more realistically expressed in musical terms than the pianoforte's Introduction?

Ex. 2

Once again I give warning regarding the semiquavers (the D sharp semiquaver in the first bar has a special meaning with its pointed proximity to the D natural in bar 2) and the rests: the short notes in 3 make an unhurried and smooth fall on to the dominant chord. On these four bars the sustaining pedal is used judiciously; after this no pedal is used—and this, in my opinion is mandatory, until bar 17, at which point hesitation is cast aside as the boy resolves to ask the brook if his heart has led him astray.

Ex.3

The sustaining pedal, changing with each half bar gives a welcome

solidarity under the voice, for here the singer's tone takes on a glow that
would have been out of keeping before. Tenderness suffuses the whole
line with an affectionate *legato*: 'Bächlein' needs a slight stress (my
mark—not Schubert's) and the first syllable of 'fragen' must have time
so that 'fr' be clearly heard. (The A sharp in the piano, as in all cases
where the consonants need time for distinct enunciation—waits for the
vowel.) 'Herz' is the high point of 19 and the gradation of tone should
make this recognized, therefore there must be no accent on 'mich' nor
too much swelling on to the high F sharp. Loveliest of phrases, we are
grateful to have it recalled in bar 21 by the pianist, who will be hard
pressed to unfold it with the smoothness and felicity of the singer.

Schubert's mark 'Very slowly' holds sway for the next eleven bars
(22–32) as the boy asks his dear companion the river 'Why are you
dumb to-day? Speak one word, just one word to me'.

Ex. 4

These two-bar phrases are modelled on the 'Ich frage' phrases at the
song's beginning but in execution they take more time and need more
control. A long steady sustained tone with a uniform *pianissimo* is
required all through this section: the triplet in 25 is deliberate against
the pianoforte's figure and should be unhurried. Emphasis is given to
'stumm'—without increase of tone—by enunciating the consonants
'st' and the accompaniment waits for this. I beg the singer not to be
afraid of the long silence in 22.

Only on 28 does the voice give more than a *pianissimo*. Schubert's >
on the 'ein' tells us he wants slightly more time on this note and the
diminuendo sign tells us that more tone is expected on it. ('One little
word'—the stress is on 'One'.)

'Yes is the word, the other No. These two words mean all the world
to me'. With simple magic the music quite suddenly changes style: the

timely ripple of the stream, the melodic pattern of the vocal line, take on a new and heightened dimension.

Ex.5

Apart from the *crescendo* and *piano* in 36 and 37 all the expression marks are mine. From 23 the pianoforte has been murmuring quietly but at 32 it comes out from behind the bushes, the last four semiquavers leading with increasing significance on to the *forte* in 33. From this point until 40 it is all recitative and the singer obeys the dictate of his heart. For my part I feel that a ringing 'Ja' (ringing that is to say, in proportion) should be dwelt on; 'heisst das eine Wörtchen' moves forward eagerly; time stands still for a moment on the ominous chord in 34 before the drawn out semiquavers leading to 'Nein', which with the accompanying harmonies, seem to embody the sharpness of death. And indeed it is to the young miller a matter of life or death for Schubert makes the following phrase the climax of the composition:

Ex. 6

die beiden Wörtchen schließen die gan-ze Welt mir ein.

This is so impassioned that the voice must rise to a *forte* at the very least. Schubert repeats the phrase we heard at 36—much more—he expands it, so important and prophetic is it to him: the singer responds unsparingly.

Block harmony prevails in the accompaniment all through this recitative section but playing of the utmost sensibility is wanted—the player anticipating the singer's every minute fluctuation of pace and nuance and never allowing a glimmer of daylight between his chords.

At 41 the heat abates with an enharmonic change on the pianoforte

Ex. 7

A slight pause forecasting the tonic chord holds us in blissful suspense before the quiet stream re-exerts its spell. Please do not mistake the *fermata* at the end of 41 for a comma; there is no break in the tone. Once again we are conscious of its soothing motion as the singer asks, 'Little stream, tell me, does my love love me?'

If I appear to have dissected this masterpiece I plead that in the whole cycle there is no more exacting a challenge. As I said earlier the singer makes us feel only the simplicity and purity of it all, miraculous simplicity to be sure. But he and his partner must have an 'eye for country' and before the first note is sounded the architecture of the song is in their minds. Nothing is left to chance. The singer who thinks 'Der Neugierige' is easy had best leave it alone: only a humble approach and a reverence for Schubert will reveal its secrets. Thus and thus only will singer and pianist find inspiration, exalt the listener and, incidentally ennoble themselves.

VII. UNGEDULD

Ungeduld, to use Richard Capell's words, is a daisy: it is a bird! The lad is transfigured with hope. At the end of each four verses comes the refrain as familiar to us as any in music: 'Thine is my heart and shall be for ever'—'These words I would carve on every tree—write on each blank page—teach a starling to sing—breathe them to the morning wind: they are written in my eyes, uttered under every breath'.

How can we account for this fantastic transfiguration from the boy's gentle melancholic mood of *Der Neugierige*? In fact in Wilhelm Müller's original sequence *Ungeduld* was preceded by a poem *Das Mühlenleben* and tells of the maid's visits to the mill and her engaging smiles. Schubert also omitted with the instinct of the great artist he was, a Prologue and Epilogue as well as two other poems. With his divine gift his muse could veer from sadness to joy with a suddenness that words could never hope to achieve.

Though joyous excitement is the key-note of the whole song the singer will look for ways and means to vary his tone according to the words. The composer gives only a *piano* sign with a few *crescendo* and *diminuendo* marks and he must expect more from us. I would suggest that the singer takes the first verse with impetuosity; the second likewise, although he should be a little less robust with his 'young starling'. (When I hear this sung too loudly I am reminded of Bottom's 'I will aggravate my voice so that I will roar you as gently as any sucking dove; I will roar you as 'twere any nightingale'.)

Verse three, 'breathing his words to the morning breeze' should be as delicate as possible. In these two middle verses 'Dein ist mein Herz' should be tempered to what has preceded this thrilling refrain. All restraint is cast aside in the final verse: the *tempo* can be quickened to add to the excitement. Only at 17 should a tight rein be reasserted to make 'und sie merkt nichts' stand out positively.

Ex. 1

und sie merkt nichts von all dem ban-gen Trei-ben:

Schubert has gone to some trouble to indicate his wishes in the Introduction.

Ex. 2

It is all lightness and grace with transparent distinction between the tip-toe *staccato* and the *legato* slurs. The ball is tossed from one hand to the other, the left predominates in the first two beats of bar 2 but on the third beat the right hand catches the ear and the player allows time for his delightful little grace note (played *before* the bass octave): bars 5 and 6 are treated likewise. The *fp* in 8 may be given fractionally more time to gain its full effect. The pianist absorbs these details into his system, takes them in his stride and plays this introduction with zest and unaffected exuberance.

A situation arises in *Ungeduld* which, since it occurs in practically every bar of the vocal part, is encountered again and again in these cycles—and indeed in many other Schubert Lieder, cannot be side-stepped.

Ex. 3

Ich schnitt' es gern in al - le Rin - den ein, ich

There it is in a nutshell. Is the voice's semiquaver to come after the pianoforte's triplet quaver or with it? The singer must determine this point one way or the other, as it occurs nearly fifty times during this strophic song's four verses. *Etwas geschwind* calls for a metronomic speed, shall we say, of ♩ = 112; faster than this the words become a jabber and it is a certainty to me that it is impossible to squeeze the proscribed semiquaver *between* the set of triplets at this pace. Some artists for whom I have the utmost admiration *think* that they sing a true semiquaver but they do not; they sing:

Ex. 4

Ich schnitt' es gern in al - le Rin -den ein

and I am all for it. In this way they make their words articulate, and no excitement is lost, moreover the singer does not get a headache.

In *Frühlingssehnsucht* (Schwanengesang) the pianist finds this:

Ex. 5

His treble is moving in triplet time, what is he to do in the second half of 44? Bearing in mind the quick movement (*Geschwind*) the semi-quaver is undoubtedly played as a triplet: try playing this otherwise and it becomes untidy and incoherent.

But I cannot claim to be consistent over the matter, I run with the hare and hunt with the hounds. In *Wasserflut* (Winterreise) we have a similar problem

Ex. 6

Man -che Trän aus mei -nen Au - gen

The semiquaver comes *after* the triplet throughout the song, not merely because it is slow moving but because it has a dragging effect giving verisimilitude to the picture of the tired wanderer half blinded by tears.

I have always played *Wasserflut* thus and no singer has ever disagreed with me; this treatment seems logical.

In *Der Atlas* it is vital that the singer having given us with iron-like rhythm at the start,

Ex. 7

Ich un - glück-sel -ger At - las,

should maintain it over the triplet accompaniment through the section
beginning at

Ex. 8

and consistently bring his semiquaver after the pianoforte's triplet. To
sing this verse turning the semiquaver into a quaver triplet alters the
rhythmic shape altogether, is out of keeping with the character of words
and music, and sounds unutterably flaccid. No, in this case it is imperative that the semiquaver is true to itself, coming after the pianoforte's
triplet. *Aufenthalt* and *Die Stadt* I put in the same category, as will be
seen later.

Summing up, I find that one cannot be arbitrary over this question.
It is undesirable to lay down rules. To allow the semiquaver and triplet
quaver to pair together is expedient where speed is involved, as in
Ungeduld and *Frühlingssehnsucht*.

By divorcing the semiquaver from the triplet quaver a disturbance is
created and this is as it should be under stress, as the suffering in
Wasserfluth or the strain in *Der Atlas*.

VIII. MORGENGRUSS

SCHUBERT SOMETIMES found C major an invigorating key. He used it in
other aubades, the two *Morgenlieder, Die frohe neubelebter Flur* (the
happy fields renewed with life) and *Eh' die Sonne früh aufersteht*

(Before an early sunrise), also in *Sängers Morgenlied, Süsses Licht* (Sweet light from golden portals) and again in the ever popular *Hark, Hark the lark* from Shakespeare's *Cymbeline*. The latter, in truth, is entitled 'Serenade' but it is none the less an apostrophe to the dawning of a joyous new day.

'Good morning, O lovely maid, why hide your head? Does my greeting displease you? Let me but gaze at your dear window from afar. Sleep-drowsy eyes why do you shrink from the sunshine? Shake off your dreams, rise fresh and free to God's bright morning'.

With some ebullience—reminding us he is still imbued with the spirit which made him declare 'Dein ist mein Herz', the miller calls up to her window 'Guten Morgen schöne Müllerin' but when he asks with less assurance (the chromatic descent in the pianoforte's bass) 'Is my greeting unwelcome?' his confidence wanes, his tone with it, leading us to the salient point of the little verse 'then must I be gone'.

Ex.1

Schubert often reserved these sublime moments as he brought a verse or song to a close. The above example is one of them. If it is performed with the feeling and understanding it deserves, one's heart is caught. The *pianissimo*, desirable enough in verses 2 and 3, is too steep a drop in the first verse; a burning longing is inherent in the very music itself and the singer communicates it with all his soul. The magical moment is enhanced by the imitation in the accompaniment's treble.

It would be a contradiction to begin Verse 2 'Let me watch your window from afar' with the same heartiness that the greeting in Verse 1 demanded, yet 'ihr blauen Morgensterne' must have fervour for the 'blue morning stars' are her eyes.

A uniform *pianissimo* prevails throughout verse 3. 'Dass ihr euch schliesst und bückt und weint' should be sung with tenderness; the singer should enjoy these words for their own sake and feel an affection for them. He should try too, to continue on to 'nach ihren stillen Wonne' without taking a breath, covering bars 14, 15, 16, 17. A tall order perhaps but it is ideally what should be done and if it can be accomplished without noticeable distress it is praiseworthy. My recommendation applies equally to the same bars in verse 4.

Finally 'Nun schüttelt ab der Träume Flor' (Shake off those shadowy dreams, rise fresh and free) resumes the vigour of the song's beginning, with an ardour that is sustained to the finish—but not at the expense of a firm *legato* line.

I would draw the singer's attention to bar 6

Ex. 2

In verse 1 the word 'Müllerin' should be sung *forte* as I have implied but were it spoken instead of sung the voice would diminish on the last two syllables. If the word were 'magical' or 'beautiful' the same principle would hold. When sung the word should be uttered just as naturally, thus the 32nd notes will be made more lissome; the same recommendation applies to the two middle verses. Regrettably these quick passing notes sometimes sound clumsy. In the final verse a distinction is made, 'Flor' needs more energy.

In bar nine the grace note is sung

Ex. 3   Ex. 4

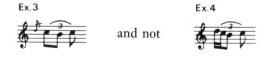

and not

IX. DES MÜLLERS BLUMEN

'THE STREAM is the friend of the miller and beside it grow blue flowers, they are the colour of my Love's eyes, I will plant them beneath her window for they know what I want so much to say to her; when her eyelids close in sleep they will whisper through her dreams "Forget me not". In the morning she will open her shutters and see the dew on these flowers, the dew of my tears.'

Morgengruss and *Des Müllers Blumen* are strophic with four verses to each song. Neither of them would have attracted special attention had it been one in the mass of Schubert's mighty miscellany, yet they play their part worthily in the cycle's picture. Moments of relief there must be, relief from highest ecstasy on one hand and the depths of depression on the other. In this song the pulse beat is normal, fervid emotion is dormant, it is therefore inadvisable to linger too long over these verses, the constant movement of the voice and pianoforte remind us that the mill-stream is in the background and it is not standing still.

The longest bars in this introduction are 3 and 4. Bar 2 is a short bar, we glide over it quickly in order to give a 'time-stress' to the first beat of 3 which is the high point of the sentence: the first beat of 4 is stressed too but to a lesser extent. We do not loiter over 5 and 6. As for the *fermata* it should be ignored in my opinion, or at least it should be of minimal duration. It is as unnecessary as the *fermata* in *Das Wandern*.

Much depends here on the handling of the vocal line.

Am Bach viel klei-ne Blu-men stehn, aus hel-len, blau-en
Au-gen sehn; der Bach, der ist— des Mül-lers Freund und

It is not worth listening to if it is not sung with utmost smoothness and if the phrase is not tapered off sensitively at 'Augen sehn'. Bar 10 wants care from the pianist for two reasons; his treble is in unison with the voice and should therefore be played very softly: also the semiquavers must be precise with the singer—who takes the first pair on 'Augen sehn' gently without haste but sings them more quickly on the sixth beat (the up beat in 10) for they do not require prominence. This is one of the moments when it may be helpful to the pianist to see the singer's lips in order to get unanimity on these semiquavers. The singer should oblige by not turning his face away from his partner. Even then the object of the exercise will be defeated if the singer is ventriloquial and does not move his lips at all; there is no virtue in that.

A wide variety of colour is not justified in this song but it will be found that each verse wants distinctive phrasing. For instance in the above example a breath is taken after 'Blumen stehn' bar 8. But in the third verse, to the same notes, we have 'Und wenn sie tät die Äuglein zu und schläft in süsser, süsser Ruh' one breath covers the whole phrase. It is obviously sung more softly than in verse one. Other instances can be found where uniformity can be avoided.

When all is said and done the Master in these years of his maturity could not put pen to paper without inscribing somewhere on the page a phrase that remains indelibly in the mind: perhaps as in 'Morgengruss' it lasts but a few moments. That is enough if it uplifts the soul.

drum sind es mei-ne Blu-

It is an endearing passage. According to Mandyczewski the *pianissimo* makes its first appearance at bar 16 (in contradiction to the *pp* coming at 7 in other editions) and if the singer caters for this it will adjust his dynamic plan. At 15 the accompanist should merge into the singer's line without let up: only in the last verse a *rallentando* adds poignancy to the singer's final 'die will ich auch euch weinen'. The marks above the vocal line are mine, a *crescendo* at 17 onto 'Blumen'—a *diminuendo* at 20 with a time-stress on the F sharp.

X. THRÄNENREGEN

UNLIKE THE two previous songs, we have here, as the saying goes 'a story-line'. *Thränenregen* is a milestone in the miller's fortunes for, having won the maid's regard, he sees now to his discomforture an ominous warning of her capriciousness. The song begins complacently and ends in misgiving.

'We sat by the river and saw the moon and the stars mirrored in it. But I—I only saw her reflection with the blue flowers nodding and lifting their eyes to her. The stream rippled merrily and seemed to call me to follow it. Then she said "It is going to rain: goodbye, I am going home".'

Schubert has a *pianissimo* in the first bar and beyond an occasional *crescendo* and *diminuendo* in the pianoforte interludes, gives no other indication of his wishes: *pp* therefore seems to prevail. Restricting

himself in this way, however, will show little imagination on the singer's
part even admitting that a delicate brush is needed. The absence—
until the final stanza—of any emotional pressure does not preclude
change of colour or added depth of tone, when the opportunity arises.

The amiable climbs and falls of the vocal line should be appreciated
especially in the first and second verses; in bars 5 to 11 it meanders up
and down but from 15 to 21 it is always rising. These nuances, I repeat,
are finespun.

Ex.1

Ex.1a

Bar 21 should be considered the high point of the verse. 'In den
silbernen Spiegel hinein' (the silvery mirror) and 'sie nickten und
blickten ihr nach' (the blue flowers nodding their heads) verse 2, should
be savoured, for they are fragrant moments for the miller.

Different treatment is needed for verse 3. 'Und in den Bach ver-
sunken der ganze Himmel schien' (all heaven seemed to be enfolded in
that stream) needs much more expansiveness—a real *forte*—at the
wonder of it all, modifying the tone at 15 as the waters ripple over the
reflected stars. But when the river calls up to him 'Follow me my
friend, follow me' this is of much significance, for one day the miller
will be obeying that call. It is brought sharply to our attention, not by
an increase in the singer's tone but by the exact reverse. It is *pianissimo*.
We make a slight *crescendo* on 'rief mit Singen und Klingen' then a
pronounced 'comma' in the vocal line before 'Geselle, Geselle, mir

nach' (21), sung so softly that it falls bewitchingly on the ear. (The pianoforte is held through the voice's silent comma—the pianist waits without lifting his sustaining pedal.)

The sudden transition to the minor causes a shiver as the miller's eyes are blurred; it should be deep toned, sung with a portentous resonance to give expression to the emotion and to give added contrast to what is to follow: 'She said "It is going to rain: good-bye, I am going home".' This blow is delivered so carelessly and unfeelingly, and with such unexpectedness that it must be thrown away by the singer: lightly sung in the most matter of fact way. He will be helped if the quaver passage in the pianoforte (28) trips down without delaying.

Ex.2

sie sprach: es kommt ein Re - gen, a - de!_ ich geh_ nach Haus.

The final phrase has no *rallentando* whatsoever—in fact it is sung as if the maid were already on her way and bidding farewell with her head hardly turned towards the boy. That the boy is hurt is clearly shown in the postlude. Once again our Schubert comes up with a telling stroke in the final bars.

Ex.3

Hope and despair are in those four bars. Hope in 33, 34: despairing realization in 35, 36. The pianist allows us to hear this dramatic change by a distinct hesitation before the minor chord, as if reluctant to accept the inevitable.

Throughout the song the pianoforte gives us the murmuring of the brook between the verses with the little undulations I have inserted.

Ex.4

In verse 3 the pianist can match the singer's increased sonority by an accentuation of the alto voice in the accompaniment

Ex. 5

Certainly if the singer decides to give more voice in the minor verse, as I advocate, his partner should anticipate this by making a *crescendo* on the last bar (24) of the interlude.

There is an ambiguity in *Thränenregen*. The *da capo* sign at the end of each verse clearly indicates that a re-statement of the introduction is intended. But in practice this introduction is never repeated: the operative word is—never. In all my experience the singer invariably re-starts at the voice's entry omitting the first four bars. According to Eric Blom (*Grove's Dictionary*) '. . . it is by no means imperative that a composer's demand for a repeat should be obeyed, but each instance of it deserves to be considered on its merits and treated as the performer thinks fit; . . . also whether any repetition is likely to try an audience's patience by excessive length or by over-familiarity with the music'.

The introduction having been played once is not heard again until the postlude where, in its last two bars, it has that dying fall into the minor.

It goes without saying that none of the verses are omitted.

XI. MEIN

UNREMITTING ENERGY from start to finish characterizes this song; energy given without stint towards one end only—the expression of triumphant joy. The melody lasting for twenty nine bars is all tonic and dominant except for one short excursion into E minor. The composer seems to have economized on his key changes so that, by taking us to a less closely related key B flat (bar 40) he can quicken our excitement when renewed vigour is wanted.

'Little stream stop your prattling, mill wheels be still, birds cease your singing. One sound alone must be heard to-day—"She is mine—mine!" Spring, are these your only blossoms? Sun, can you shine no brighter? O, then I alone seem to understand that blessed word "Mine".'

Ex.1

In this prelude and throughout the song every note has an animation of its own. The fluidity we heard in *Das Wandern, Wohin, Halt*, to which the sustaining pedal contributed so effectively, bears no relation to the playing required here. If a violinist were performing this figure he would give each quaver a separate bow; in so far as he can, the pianist employs a similar touch: he plays *non-legato* but with the sustaining pedal. Despite the *diminuendo* on the treble's quaver groups the two chords are played with relish.

Where, metaphorically, *Ungeduld* can be said to trip along on its toes—*Mein* clatters along with the assurance of a stalwart Arcadian lad who has made his conquest.

The singer's entry in the very first song of the cycle was made impatiently. So it is here; he cannot wait to allow the crotchet rest its full value—he is bursting to start. Although 'mässig geschwind' is the indication, we must feel only two beats to the bar (it is marked *alla breve* in Mandyczewski) so the metronome speed is not less than 96 = ♩.

I feel the *pianissimo* in the accompaniment at bar 9, to which I refer later, is too much of an understatement: it certainly does not apply to the singer.

Almost every bar is melismatic in this song giving the singer openings for many intrusive H's if enthusiasm runs away with technical control. He is to be admired if he appreciates the importance, no matter how boisterous his spirits, of fine *legato* singing over and contrasting with the pianoforte's *martellato*.

'Reim allein' is sung four times in the course of the song and must always be shaped in the same way. I suggest the grace note be treated thus:

There are three steps up (A, B, C) example 2, sung with mounting ardour but always with a reserve of power to make the eight bars beginning at 30 the climax of this verse;

the above phrase is repeated—almost identically—with those F sharps ringing triumphantly.

Only two phrases in the entire song seem to cry out for a broadening of the *tempo*, the first one ushers in the B flat section 38, 39, 40.

Again we have steps in this fresh section bars 41 to 46, climbing up as did bars 9 to 15: 'Frühling, sind das alle deine Blümelein? Sonne, hast du keinen hellern schein'? Spring's flowers and sun's radiance are held up almost to scorn; 'Frühling' and 'Sonne' are each being hailed and those two words must be thrown out with joyous emphasis.

Very few melodies are self-sufficient and even Schubert's depend for their full and life-enhancing realization on the harmonies and counter melodies in the pianoforte parts. By itself the following looks rather matter-of-fact

but when embraced by the accompaniment, it becomes full of meaning, has a cutting edge.

In such moments as these the accompanist must spend himself as generously as his partner.

We take leave of the B flat section with a second and last broadening at 59, 60 where the turn—I write it out in full—is taken with deliberation.

At 60 the pianist picks up the *tempo* immediately—makes a big *crescendo* 61, 62, 63 and drops to a sudden *piano* at the voice's entry at 64.

I am as much in agreement with this *piano* at the return to the subject at 64 as I am against the *pp* at bar 9. Schubert not infrequently asks for *pp* in his accompaniments where a healthy *mezzo-forte* would seem more desirable. Can it be that he was influenced by Johann Michael Vogl where dynamic notation was concerned? Schubert was somewhat in awe of this famous singer who was twice his age and who did so much to promote his songs. He would certainly value Vogl's opinion. Being an accompanist himself Schubert was naturally modest.

XII. PAUSE

THE MILLER gazes at his lute hanging on the wall, uncertain whether to be happy or sad. 'My heart is too full' he says 'I can find no rhyme for my song: a cheerful song tells naught of the pain of my longing, nor can anything I sing carry the surfeit of my joy. So rest, dear lute, on this nail. When a breeze stirs the green riband across your strings or a bee brushes them with its wings, I tremble and ask myself if this is an echo of love's pain or a prelude to new songs.'

In the whole cycle there is nothing more subtle than *Pause*. It is something of a paradox with the miller complaining he cannot sing, yet doing so in the most poignant way. He finds solace it seems, by sinking his strains beneath the haunting *ostinato* of the accompaniment but ever and anon, as if he can hold himself in check no longer, breaks out in expressions pregnant with longing. We find this in the first nineteen bars where the voice is largely an *obligato* to the pianoforte's motif save for a momentary rise at 15–16, 'Ich kann nicht mehr singen, mein Herz ist so voll'. This is the general geography of the song.

There is a tendency to take too slow a pace: it is marked *Ziemlich geschwind* (somewhat quickly) and my metronomic suggestion is 96 = ♪ as a basic *tempo* although we shall not be anchored to this inexorably.

Ex.1

Bars 1 and 2 are subdued, 3 is the longest bar of this prelude being the high point and it should sing keenly: 4 sinks down. Bars 7–8 connote a philosophical resignation to me (which I shall hope to explain at the end of my homily) and should not be lingered over.

All the grace notes in the example above come before the beat. Later at 11, 14, 19 these small notes come with the beat.

I give bar 14 as an example (rather than 11 or 19) because the singer here must allow the pianoforte's grace notes to be cleared before he takes his own: it is advisable to allow more time for this; it prevents any ruffling of the quiet mood and it gives more impact to the *crescendo* on 'Ich kann nicht mehr singen'.

The climax of the song (not emotionally but dynamically) is reached during bars 20–40.

'Sehnsucht' could not be expressed with more meaning than that. The pianist feels it keenly as he did in bar 3 of his prelude, and the singer emerges from his musing and responds with less restraint.

'How great is the weight of a happiness that cannot be expressed in song?'

The *fortissimo* on 'Ei' is Schubert's and it is surprising. Certainly a change of colour is demanded here and a new emphasis; but the singer may well feel that the long rising phrase should be ushered in with less violence. And yet this aspiring climb is impeded by the *pianissimo* 35. Both the latter sign and the *fortissimo* are authentic though their juxtaposition seems excessive. Without doubt the passage climbs from 33 to 37 and falls from 38 to 40, if the singer wishes to draw this line clearly he can temporize in the way I have marked. My suggestions—including fluctuation of speed—are above the stave.

Now the accompaniment takes us back to the quiet contemplation of the opening bars, but a lifting of the vocal line at 52, 53 (compare it with 15, 16) takes us to G minor and thence to C minor 'und es durchschauert mich'

Ex.6

Bar 55, 'es durchschauert mich' ('sends a shiver through me') badly needs that *diminuendo* and the *fermata*, not only for their immediate effect but in preparation for the most magical moments that are now coming in the key of A flat.

Ex.7

'Why did I let the green ribbon hang so long?' The time stress on the third beat of each bar (not an accent) must be observed but within the *pianissimo*. It should be remembered that the terms 'softly' and 'slowly' are not synonymous and the *Ziemlich geschwind* is resumed: in fact 'Warum' is the linchpin of the song's basic *tempo*. There is a natural speech-rhythm to this word and it should be sung as spoken. (There is sometimes a key-phrase or such a word as this in a song, with an intrinsic rhythm of its own; it has to be sought.)

From 63–79 (embracing two bars of the postlude) singer and pianist have *carte blanche*. It is all recitative and is abundantly suggestive alternatively of optimism and pessimism, the promise of high hope, the dread of vain expectation. We are reminded of the leading question in *Der Neugierige* 'Is it Yes—or No' and of a similar suspense in the postlude of *Thränenregen.*

Perplexed by the soft sighs uttered by his lute he asks

Ex. 8

The change to the minor at 63 is portentous and the pianist takes much time over it with a significant wait on the second beat before engulfing us in the F flat major chord. His playing of this can be of enormous help to his partner who waits before his entry until this marvellous chord has been absorbed and then he puts his question in his own time. If he is forced to breathe after *Nachklang* he should take it deliberately, not a snatched breath. It is all *pianissimo* as befits the sombre uncertainty of the mood. But 'soll es das Vorspiel neuer Lieder sein' (again with a decided break after the *fermata* in 66) strikes a new chord with a reassuring return to the tonic key as the singer infects us with his optimism. (The expression marks in the above example are mine.)

The freedom the singer enjoys in his recitative section should be continued in the postlude. Once again it echoes the perplexity of the singer.

The third and fourth beats are the longest in these bars. After each bar I have inserted an extra half beat as an indication to the player that there is a space between each utterance. This space or silence is vital between the *mezzoforte* major 78 and the *pianissimo* minor in 79.

The last two bars 80–81 duplicating bars 7–8 of the introduction should be played in time, almost throwing them away.

This postlude summarizes the whole song and is deserving of some thought. At 78 hope is in the ascendant; at 79 on the wane. I suggested earlier that 80–81 signified resignation. It is as if the young lover, after weighing up the question shrugs his shoulders and says with a sigh 'Ah, well, who knows?'

XIII. MIT DEM GRÜNEN LAUTENBANDE

'"What a shame to see that green ribbon fade on the wall, I am so fond of green." So you spoke, sweetheart, and straightway I untie it and send it to you, for I, the white miller, am fond of green. Ever green is our love, green are our hopes; bind your hair with this ribbon and I shall know where hope and love have their dwelling.'

Every phrase in this dear little song is fragrant with happiness. It is tender in feeling, yet sprightly with its octave skips in the pianoforte and its drops of sixths and sevenths in the vocal line.

A *mezzoforte* is desirable here. The quaverchords in the bass (2) are
not prolonged, so that the jubilant figure in the treble is made evident.

As for the trite chord which *introduces* the introduction, I wish it did
not exist.

This song is so short and gay that the singer will not be worried by
his inability to make one verse any different from the others. A speed of
♩ = 120 sends it along pleasantly and lightly. The brisk pace is arrested
by the *fermata* on 7:

Ex. 2

and at 10 and 18 a slight slowing down is desirable to enable the 32nd
(demisemiquaver) chord in the accompaniment to come after the semiquaver in the voice part. The singer should show consideration here for
the pianist.

Minute fluctuations of pace add zest. The semiquavers in 14 should be
hastened up to the second beat—and to this the pianist responds by
hurrying his (bar 15) semiquavers: the singer catches him without
hesitation.

Ex. 3

'Ist auch dein ganzer Liebster weiss' in verse 2 is clearly articulated.
Only twice in the cycle does the miller allude to the white floury dust, the
trade mark, literally, of his employment: here the allusion is playful
enough—later it is used self-pityingly.

I must add a postscript by way of expiation for my effrontery in wanting to abolish the solid B flat chord in bar 1.

In my *Singer and Accompanist* (Eyre Methuen) I wrote a short essay on Haydn's 'She never told her love . . . She sat like patience on a monument smiling at grief'. The majestic pianoforte introduction of fourteen bars has, like this Schubert song, a long preliminary tonic chord: I wrote 'The song really begins at bar 2 and I have never understood the necessity for that chord in bar 1.' A critic whom I respect told me 'That chord—long held—expresses the movelessness of that monument and is most significant'. I see the logic of this. Perhaps, therefore, that chord at the beginning of *Mit dem grünen Lautenbande* has a special meaning that I have not yet comprehended. None the less, in our latest recording Fischer-Dieskau and I omitted it.

XIV. DER JÄGER

A RIVAL now appears on the scene who seems to have unlimited shooting and fishing rights: it is the hunter, a man to be hated and feared. By comparison with the dusty miller he is a picturesque figure with his weather-beaten complexion, his guns and his dogs. Our young lover feeling at a disadvantage is filled with jealous misgivings and in this song he bursts into an angry tirade saying there is no game here, only his own precious doe. He bids the hunter be gone. 'If you would find favour with my darling, trim that grizzly beard; shoot the wild boar that roots in her kitchen garden.'

I think this harangue is the expression of a shy and sensitive man's thoughts, not a confrontation; the rough-hewn hunter would not have found the words particularly provocative. It is Schubert rather than Müller who stirs the blood, for the words, considering the hatred consuming the miller, do not convey anything like the venom that the music does. For sixtyfour bars without one moment's relaxation the song throbs with feverish pressure with the brassy suggestion of the hunting horn in the accompaniment.

Ex.1

At the first note of this introduction, though it is marked *mezzoforte*, the listener must be struck by the harshness of sound; for the pianist does not seek a beautiful tone. If there is ever a reason for playing with stiffness of finger it is here; there are no nuances, no curves, it is unrelenting hardness. The *Geschwind* marking I take to be ♩.= 96 and the *staccato* is to be observed; the pianist may remove his foot from the vicinity of the sustaining pedal throughout the song. He reduces his tone in bars 5 and 9 so as not to cover the voice when it is low in the stave. The *staccato* sign in the first bar of the introduction is not directed solely to the pianist for the vocal line is *non-legato* moving in two-bar phrases and it is all to the good if a breath is taken between each phrase: the words 'hier' and 'Revier' for instance are snapped off. To endeavour to sing in a pleasant well-modulated voice would be the quintessence of folly: the mood of the miller and the shape and substance of the music call for an acrid or steely tone.

It might help the singer in rehearsal to think of a nasal quality—though I suggest this with hesitation—in order to get the snarling colour which is essential.

The mounting steps from 13 to 28 add fuel to the flame of the miller's temper: the singer caters for this by reducing tone—without making it obvious—at the beginning of each ascent and loudening as he gets to the top.

Ex.2

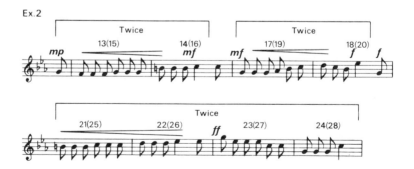

If he does not make this reduction in volume before each climb, passion will be dissipated. *Reculer pour mieux sauter*. The pattern of two-bar phrases is broken at 21 by a repeated four-bar phrase—the apex of the climb, and this the singer affirms by sweeping over these bars (21–24) in one breath and similarly bars 25–28. Each voice in the three part harmony of the pianoforte is of equal importance save from 13–22 where the *alto* moving in contrary motion to the vocal line must predominate slightly over the others.

Ex.3

The postlude is the same as bars 1–4, with the final bar played in time—inflexibly, as much as to say 'a curse on you'.

Eifersucht und Stolz follows immediately with only a few seconds break between the two songs.

XV. EIFERSUCHT UND STOLZ

Eifersucht und Stolz (Jealousy and Pride) is desperate and all the more so by reason of its impotence. Impotent because the full realization that all is lost pierces the heart and mind of the boy, and because he is helpless to do anything about it. For the first and only time he speaks harshly of the girl to the stream, cries shame on her for her infidelity. 'Whither so fast and wild, dear stream, are you tracking down the bold hunter? First, turn about, and scold the miller's daughter for her light wantonness.'

A picture of the tossing angry waters, matching the mood of the lad and flowing more madly than ever before, is depicted in the introduction. Immediately we are taken to the core of the miller's trouble.

Ex.1

The pianist's foot, rested all through 'Der Jäger', now comes into play again, for the sustaining pedal generously used, adds to the surging waves of sound; every savage semiquaver should be heard, also the heavy throb in the bass. In the vocal line too, each semiquaver must be distinct and if the song is taken at excessive speed the palpitating rhythm will go for nothing: it is marked *Geschwind* and I take the tempo to be ♩ = 120 (Schubert seldom wrote *Sehr Geschwind*: if he wanted quickness of tempo he contented himself by writing *Schnell* as he does in *Erlkönig* and *Rastlose Liebe*).

Much is made of the distracted cries 'Kehr um' (turn about)

Jealousy brings out the worst in a man and at 27 for nine bars this is made evident. 'Did you see her last evening standing at her gate, craning her neck to catch a glimpse of him?'

It is a querulous aside ('mit langem Halse' with craning neck) is almost sneeringly uttered with its high F's and octave drop. The pianist makes a *diminuendo* in 25–26 to help the singer reduce his voice to a 'conspiratorial' level.

These eleven bars, while still picturing the fast flowing current, are transitional and lead to a new section where the structure of the music is abruptly and strikingly changed.

'When the hunter returns from the chase—it is unseemly for a nice girl to be on the look-out for him.'

Schubert has a *mezzoforte* here so that at 39 and 43 we hear in the accompaniment the hunting horn, a sound that has become an obsession with the miller and it needs the same unyielding touch that was required in *Der Jäger*. While the singer is the jaundiced lover, it is the pianist who is the hunter and his playing should be square and insensitive: the sustaining pedal is unwanted in these bars.

It is in this outburst that the singer will find the key to the true tempo of the entire song. 'Wenn von dem Fang' etc. is sung at the same speed that it would be spoken and I find as aforesaid that $\quad = $ 120 meets the case.

Now the miller, as if his anger had made him forget he was talking to the stream, turns back to it 'Geh, Bächlein hin und sag ihr das' (Go millstream and tell her that).

Ex.5

We are conscious again of the running water. As these words are uttered the music also turns back, not to the tonic G minor but surprisingly to the major. Taken out of its context this appears lighthearted, but that is certainly not its message: rather it would imply that the miller is deriving a perverse pleasure at the pain he is inflicting on himself in this castigation of the girl he loves. It is an idea re-inforced by the next and last section where the rejected lover, motivated by pride actually does simulate cheerfulness or at least indifference at the girl's defection.

'But do not breath a word about my sad face. Tell her I fashioned a reed into a pipe and am playing merry tunes for the children to sing and to dance.'

Ex.6

The secret message, admitting the sadness reflected in his face— again in an aside—is sung *pianissimo* and the pace is slackened at 'traurigen Gesicht' (sad face) so that it really means what it says. At

64, however, the quick tempo must be resumed and maintained until the end.

'Sag ihr's' (Tell her) repeated ten times has even more bitterness than its parallel—the insistent 'Kehr um' of the first verse.

Ex. 7

As the miller sheds all pretence, these reiterations become frenzied, so much so that the postlude is infected, its closing chords being smashed out with undiminished speed and increased violence.

XVI. DIE LIEBE FARBE

THERE FOLLOWS in Wilhelm Müller's original lyrics *Erster Schmerz, letzter Schmerz* wherein the miller tells us that behind those brightly shining window panes, the maiden whom he adores is embracing his hated rival. Fortunately Schubert with his impeccable taste omitted this poem: we have seen the poor lad torn to pieces already. Enough is enough, Schubert liked to leave a little to the imagination.

Die liebe Farbe is numb with despair. The boy is in a trance and scarcely knows what he is saying.

'I will wear the green willow, seek a cyprus grove and rosemary. My love is so fond of green.

'I will go a-hunting, the game I hunt is death. My love is so fond of hunting.

'Dig me a grave and cover it with green turf. My love is so fond of green.'

Usually in a strophic song the singer looks for ways and means whereby he can vary his tone colour, his rhythm or phrasing according to the sense of the words. This is a laudable routine, generally, but the singer who puts this precept into practice in *Die liebe Farbe* misunderstands the song. It is to be sung without any attempt to underline or 'colour' the words, without any well-tempered nuances. The miller is hardly more aware of the significance of what he is saying than poor mad Ophelia— 'at his head a grass-green turf, at his heels a stone'. Even the dim idea of the hunt and its association with the man who has supplanted him does not rouse the boy from his torpor. His mind seems fixed on one theme 'mein Schatz hat's grün so gern' (my love loves green) murmured over and over again; he says it without emotion, he says it almost mechanically and because of this it conveys a world of sadness.

And yet there is something else that seems to penetrate into his consciousness, something that hammers away, softly but unremittingly, and says 'Death' to him.

Ex.1

All intensity resides in the piano part centred on the ever repeated F sharp—played over five hundred times in the course of the song. Except for the *fp* chords in 16 and in the penultimate bar of the postlude the accompaniment rarely rises above the level of a *piano*, mostly it is *pianissimo*. But within this narrow range the player puts all the imagination and feeling possible into his solo bars; he will be playing these four times—before each verse and at the end—and they must not, unlike the voice part, be treated in a listless way.

Ex.2

Only here can the player depart from the steady undeviating pulse which will be required when we arrive at bar 5. There are time stresses on the first beats of 2, 3 and 4, each imperceptibly taking a little more time than the last—and with only the slightest increase in tone. Such delicacy of touch has not been called for since *Der Neugierige.*

Ex.3

The bass in the accompaniment is always moving with the voice. Those nagging F sharps are in a separate world of their own.

Any animation—in spirit not in speed—that the second verse might suggest ('Wohl auf dem fröhlichen Jagen') is made by the pianist with a hint of the hunting horn. The final verse is softest of all.

These minute variations of colour are only for the pianist to consider.

It has been said that the strophic form Schubert has adopted for *Die liebe Farbe* accords with the first of the three stanzas but is inapt for the second and the third. If Wilhelm Müller had heard this song he might have agreed with the criticism. Possibly he conceived a dramatic manifestation. But in this case one must ask which is the more profound work of art, the poetry or the music? There is only one answer. Schubert could possibly have considered a pretentious setting to these homely little verses had he not omitted *Erster Schmerz, letzter Schmerz,* but coming as it does between two tempestuous songs, *Die liebe Farbe* fits perfectly into the architecture of the cycle.

The great musician possibly saw more clearly into the young miller's mind, felt more acutely the pain in his heart than the poet.

Although the interest of harmony and texture is sustained by the pianoforte, it remains a framework for the melancholy disclosure the singer is making. My suggestion that the voice part should be executed without colour or pronounced nuances does not make the singer's task any easier—quite the reverse. The top F sharps for instance—there are four in each verse—must not be made 'of great moment'. In bars 19, 20 'Mein Schatz hat's grün so gern', it is 'gern' that is the softest note; admittedly the same phrase in 10, 11 is marked with a rise and fall but this is very slender. Only at 16 is there a *fp* and the wise singer will let his partner take most of the responsibility for it.

XVII. DIE BÖSE FARBE

'I would that I could go out into the wide world, if only everything were not so green; green woods and fields! I would I could tear off those leaves and wash the grass pale with my tears. O green, you hateful colour, you mock the poor white miller.'

The boy is in a ferment. We can hear by the agitation of the introduction and the rapid alternation of major and minor that he has thrown off the cloaking lethargy of *Die liebe Farbe*. All his hatred is centred on the odious colour green, the hue of the hunter's tunic.

Die böse Farbe is turbulent and yet it is related to the previous song, we are constantly reminded of that prodding, relentless repeated note, we hear the horn of the hunter, and, as in *Die liebe Farbe*, not one word of obloquy is directed at the maid; only in his temper—*Eifersucht und Stolz*—did he speak ill of her. There is even a connection in tempo. The metronomic beat is ♩ = 63, twice the speed of the slower song which should be ♪ = 63. The tempi I advocate are approximate. *Ziemlich geschwind* (rather quick) is the instruction, but if the singer wishes for more speed the pianist will be hard put to it to cope with all his repeated chords especially in the second half of the song. There are two beats to the bar not four.

Ex.1

As usual in moments of impetuosity the singer's semiquaver entry, rather than delayed, is precipitated and we are swept up to the *fortissimo* 'Welt hinaus'.

(A word must be said, with respect, in regard to the composer's indications; knowing how Schubert shunned profusion we find their lack a little too economical in this song. In Ex. 1. for instance, the pianist will find Schubert's *diminuendo* easier to achieve in bars 1 and 2 if he makes a slight *crescendo* in the first half of each bar as I indicate above the stave. Again in bar 5 it is surprising to find a *forte* for the voice when the accompaniment is given a *fortissimo*: this, like the *pianissimo* in 32 which incredibly holds sway till the song's end, is to be regarded as an oversight and must be adjusted by the performers. I am afraid also that the *subito fortissimo* on the last syllable of 'Totenbleich' bar 20 is not feasible; if this instruction were obeyed the sudden and totally unexpected salvo would make the listener leap out of his seat, it needs a preparatory *crescendo*.)

A decided contrast in tone is wanted between the formidable attack bars 5–8 and the retreat at 9–12. In the first phrase the miller declares 'I would . . .' and follows it with 'If only . . .'.

Bars 17 and 18 are *piano* with the recommended *crescendo* on 19 leading to 'Totenbleich' (pale as death) which deserves a *fortissimo* and is, so far, the climax.

Ex. 2

After this outburst a decrease in tone, a falling away of emotional intensity is natural and leads to the distressing cry 'Green, you mock the poor white miller'.

Ex.3

So anxious will the singer be to put all the pitifulness he can into these bars, the short stabbing exclamations and the deflated 'weissen Mann', that he may wish to hold back the tempo slightly. We shall appreciate more clearly what he is saying if he does so.

At 32 to the words 'I would lie before her door in storm, rain and snow, softly singing the one word "Farewell" ', the music of the opening bars is duplicated but understandably sung more softly: the anatomy of both the vocal line, with its soaring phrases, and the accompaniment, set in the most resonant register of the pianoforte, do not seem to accommodate a *pianissimo*, the performers should get as near as they can to this level notwithstanding.

But it is from 41–48 that it will be found impossible to adhere to the *pp* laid down in 32. 'When the hunting horn sounds in the forest, her window will open, but she will not be looking out for me.'

Ex.4

The three-part writing in the pianoforte is intended, surely, as an echo of *Der Jäger*, it is fashioned in the same rhythm, same *staccato*, has a similar brassy quality. The hard tone he dug from his instrument must be called to mind by the player but not put into execution, for the percussive nature of these bars should be modified as far as possible, since the horn tone is not immediate—it is reminiscent. Here too the message has a deeper meaning than that of the irascible *Der Jäger*: those repeated notes have been harassing the poor miller, off and on, since bar 22 and remind him of that tragical whisper of death heard in *Die liebe Farbe*.

If the performers find themselves unable to keep this 'hunting section' down to a *pianissimo* they need feel no dismay. They will treat it as considerately as they can knowing they are leading us now to the song's soul-stirring conclusion.

'O untwine that green ribbon from your brow. Farewell, farewell, give me your hand in parting.'

In *Am Feierabend* (Ex. 3) 'Why is my arm so weak?' the singer was asked to give an impression of breathlessness. Technically the above phrase is approached in the same way, but of course it is a thousand times more anguished. The miller seems suffocated by his emotion and yet his cries of 'Ade, ade,' gain a little in strength through sheer desperation, for the girl will never touch his hand. The turbulence of the streaming accompaniment reflects his tormented mind.

Being in the form of a rondo (*a b a c a*) we hear the subject thrice and the words make it incumbent on the singer to vary his tone-colour each time he sings it. This final return to the tune is most moving of all and the first 'farewells' (52, 53, 54) are sung with a full heart but no louder than *mezzoforte*.

In Example 6, with the realization that 'this is forever' the singer begins at 'reiche mir' (57) his long *diminuendo*, and continues it to the very last note.

The closing 'zum Abschied deine Hand' I have rarely heard performed as it deserves to be; there is nothing difficult technically about it to the insensitive singer, who will lapse into a matter-of-fact *mf* and rob the phrase of all emotional significance, but to sing it with understanding and poetic feeling then indeed it becomes difficult; tear-choked retrospect is in the music: a stretching out despairingly for a grain of regard—let alone sympathy—which is denied.

This song abounds in spasmodic changes of mood. An effect or colour (see Ex. 5) may last only for a few bars and then convulsively shift to a new one. Enormous demands are made here on the singer's flexibility of mind and voice and depth of feeling.

I might attempt at this juncture to give the pianist a little help. The section shown in Ex. 4 extends for eight bars and is to be played with clearest articulation. Now we see the reason for Schubert's instruction *ziemlich geschwind—(somewhat* quickly): if we begin the song too fast the pianist will be unable to cope with those repeated chords when he comes to them. Such passages last sometimes for a few phrases, sometimes for a page or more. This is the moment, with the pianist at the end of his tether, that the singer with uncanny instinct will suggest that we now increase the speed. You can depend on it. I therefore suggest the following fingering to ease the situation.

Ex.7

A comparison with example 4 will show that the notes are the same but have been re-distributed.

XVIII. TROCKNE BLUMEN

THE LAST manifestation of happiness or peace of mind was *Mit dem grünen Lautenbande* number thirteen in the cycle. Since then each song has told of anger, bitter jealousy, or has seen the boy crushed and despairing. Wilhelm Müller had four more songs to come in his original set, all pertaining to the woe of the unhappy miller, and at this point preceding *Trockne Blumen*, he had some heart-sick stanzas about forget-me-nots called *Blümlein Vergissmeinnicht*. Schubert evidently found this excessive and he left it out. Indeed so moving are the three magical songs bringing this cycle to a close that it must be confessed the inclusion of yet one more would have been a little too much.

In this song the lover tells the withered flowers she gave to him, they must lie in his grave; though wet with his tears they will, like love which is dead, never bloom again.

Sentimental? Perhaps. But the superior smile vanishes on hearing how Schubert has adorned these verses with his matchless genius.

Ex.1

Ziemlich langsam

Ihr Blüm-lein al - le, die sie mir gab, euch soll man le - gen mit mir ins Grab. Wie seht ihr al - le mich

an— so— weh, als ob ihr wüß-tet, wie mir ge-scheh?

Against the detached accompaniment's chords—chords dry as a dead branch—the voice has the smoothest possible *legato*. The semi-quavers are as important as the quavers, in every instance there must be a feeling of profundity about them; they are not louder than the quavers but each one is held as long as the singer dare hold it without disturbing the inevitability of the funereal march movement.

The keen moments at 14, 15, 'Why so wet?' stand out by reason of the sustained F sharp of the voice, by the modulation to B major which, promised for several bars is now settled, by reason of the pianoforte coming to life and echoing the singer's question.

Ex. 2

wo - von   so naß? ——

But a variation on the above comes at 28, to the words 'the flowers she gave me'.

Ex. 3

die Blüm-lein al - le, die sie   mir gab.

Only a trifling change is made in notation between 14 and 28 but it contains a world of meaning. For argument's sake if 'die sie mir gab' were sung to the notation of 14 (and I recommend the singer to experiment for his own satisfaction) we should be unmoved. But now as it is at 28 with 'She' made the high point, the poignancy of it cannot be lost.

As I said earlier the miller harbours no bitterness towards the maid who has been false to him. How can he? He loves her. We see it in the last verse as he says 'But when she passes my mound and says in her heart "He was true to me" then all you flowers spring up, for May has come and winter is over'.

> My dust would hear her and beat,
> Had I lain for a century dead;
> Would start and tremble under her feet,
> And blossom in purple and red.

The overwhelming and single-hearted passion concentrated in Tennyson's lines is hardly matched by Müller's Arcadian verse but the miller lad was scorched by the same fire. Schubert felt it and expressed the consolatory suggestion by putting the last stanza to a gentle rocking movement—celestial and spell-binding. Its waving rhythm and mesmeric effect presage the final song *Des Baches Wiegenlied* (The brook's lullaby) and is, incidentally in the same key.

Ex.4

- aus, her-aus! der Mai   ist kom-men, der Win - ter ist aus.

In this new section there is more to appreciate than the mere fact
that we move from the minor to the major. The psyche has been transfigured from death to life; withered flowers breathe again, darkness
yields to light. The love-lorn boy conjures up a visionary spring he will
never enjoy yet it gives him a spiritual elation and the music smiles.

Vocal line and violoncello-like bass are knit in a most intimate
ensemble. It was suggested in the minor movement that the semiquavers should not be lightly treated. Now, however, with a different
rhythmic pattern there is a desirable stress on each beat of every bar and
the semiquavers, though by no means parenthetical, are noticeably
lighter than before.

'And says in her heart "He was true to me"' (33–34, 42–43) deserves
much consideration: this phrase is the kernel of the whole situation.
This is what it is all about. The miller is not asking for much. Herein is
summed up all his sweetness of nature, his lack of bitterness and his
humility.

It will be found that a slight break in the tone (without breathing)
after 'Herzen' helps to make 'der meint es treu' infinitely tender. In
fact the semiquaver 'der' is the high point and is imperceptibly lingered
on.

The *pp* at 30 is maintained until 35 and here the singer, urged by the
fp in the accompaniment, starts a *crescendo* leading to an outspoken
forte at 'der Mai ist kommen' (May has come).

These nine delectable bars are repeated and then Schubert, by no
means anxious to discontinue the spell, adds a short coda.

Ex.5

It is as if the miller, momentarily exultant, were saying 'O Grave! where is thy victory?' The singer makes this the climax of the composition and keeps to his *forte* to the very end of bar 51. There is a broadening of tempo at 'Winter ist aus' but it is to be made with good judgement so as not to put the accompaniment too much out of stride, for the swaying figure continues in the postlude in the major key for two bars and then, to remind us that visions are but transitory, leads us back to the minor; the minor key of the dead flowers.

Ex.6

Though *pp*, the bass continues to be the solo voice and the penultimate B sings on after the right hand chord has been released; this necessitates a considerable *rallentando*. I have slightly altered the notation on the last chord of 56 to make my meaning clear.

XIX. DER MÜLLER UND DER BACH

SINCE WE last heard the ruffled waters in *Eifersucht und Stolz* the stream seems to have been forgotten by the miller: now with his broken heart he turns once more to the one companion that has been constant to him throughout his course.

The little song (the adjective is not intended pejoratively) is so simple, with sentiments so naïve that it is beyond understanding why it should move us as it does. Other composers hold us spellbound by their magic, but the rationale of that magic can be explained. What was Schubert's secret? We are forever marvelling and forever mystified.

This is a colloquy between the boy and the millstream. The boy says 'When a true heart dies for love the lilies fade, the moon—lest men see her tears—veils herself, and the little angels cover their eyes too, and sobbing, sing the soul to rest'.

Ex.1

Wo ein treu-es Her-ze in Lie - be ver-geht, da wel - ken die
Li - lein auf je - dem Beet;

Clear and gentle tones are needed for the first minor section. No striving after conventional rises and falls or subtle nuances should be attempted nor any *crescendo* made up to the F sharp 'Liebe' in bar 5; the pain is expressed by the discordant E flat in the accompaniment. The verse is in four-bar groups and no breaths are taken save where a rest is marked. The vocal timbre is attenuated, even anaemic: paradoxically the singer must have technical mastery to achieve this effect for the voice must be well supported and the delivery smooth. One bears in mind that the boy, mentally and physically, has got to the end of his tether and the more the singer can convince us of this, the greater will be the contrast when we turn to the major key where the brook endeavours to comfort the broken heart.

Ex. 2

The Brook: 'When love loosens itself from sorrow a new star twinkles in the sky: then three unfading roses, red and white, spring up from a thorny branch and little wingless angels come down to earth'.

Henceforth the calm waters in the accompaniment flow on until the end. From this point until bar 60 there is more animation. (Wolf would have labelled it *nicht schleppend*).

There are eighty bars of singing in this song and the four-bar phrase is unvaried. Wonder to relate, we are not aware of any tedium. All the same the singer with a lively imagination can quicken our interest; at 33–34 for instance he should observe the commas at 'ein Sterlein, ein neues', not of course, by breathing at these punctuations but by making a slight break in the tone. Before 'Himmel erblinkt' (39) however he may need a breath, for this bar is sung with repose, is allowed plenty of space.

Ex.3

At 41 the right hand while always *piano* has life and movement and is played without laziness and with gentle *non legato* touch; any fear of skittishness will be obviated by the sustaining pedal—changed in every bar. It is almost sprightly in feeling and has a ripple inspired by the singer's 'da springen drei Rosen'; above this ripple the vocal line is smooth.

Ex.4

Where can the singer breath? If he breathes after 'Dornenreis' (48) it will mar the smoothness of the line and will inevitably be a snatched affair coming between two semiquavers. Ideally he should take 47–52 in one confident sweep, taking his breath after 'wieder', curtailing without making it obvious, the last syllable of that word. Should this step be adopted, the suggestion made above for a quicker tempo will not be unwelcome, but to hasten the passage in order to contain it in one span would be a shame, far better if a breath is necessary to take it after 'Schneiden', bar 50.

Five top G's appear in this second stanza (34, 38, 46, 54, 58) and there must be no fuss over them, they are not made more important by reason of their pitch. In fact 'Sternlein' (Ex. 2) has more weight than 'neues'; the first syllable of 'Morgen' (bar 54) has more bias than the second syllable.

So we arrive at the boy's last words; he has come to his brook for comfort and he knows his only peace is in its embrace, in its quiet cool depths.

The Miller: 'Ah, little stream, dear stream, you mean so well, but do you know how Love wounds? Ah, below, below is cool peace. Little stream, sing on, sing on'.

The expectation of assuagement of all his pain is expressed in these words of the boy. He utters them softly to be sure, but with an underlying resolve necessitating a firm vocal line that is quite unlike the mournful debility which characterized the first verse.

The pianist makes the change from the major really profound with his minor third in bar 61. At this point too we are gradually eased into the slower tempo of the song's beginning though always mindful of the gentle movement of the water.

At bar 68 to the words 'do you know what Love does?'

Ex.5

we hear again the same rhythmical figure of bar 39 as if to remind us of the relationship between brook and boy.

'Down below I shall find peace' is *pianissimo*, this is obligatory (the singer observes the C natural in 73 as opposed to the C sharp at bar 13); but the words 'Little stream sing on' are sung twice and there are different ways of singing them.

Ex.6

Bäch-lein, lie-bes Bäch-lein, so sin-ge nur zu

Let us consider 75 to 78 sung so quietly that we have to strain our ears to hear—then 79 to 81 sung with a swelling heart, a more generous tone, as if the boy, taking his last glance at the trees and fields clasps all nature to his breast. The marvellous change from B flat to G major is made the more soothing by its lack of effusiveness.

Alternatively let us reverse the procedure by giving more tone from 75 to 78 subsequently dying away as the singer finishes.

I am obviously undecided which of these choices I prefer. Perhaps after all the singer should wait for the inspiration of the moment of performance.

We are reminded in the postlude that the brook sang of a new star twinkling in the sky (EX. 2 bar 35) and this surely implies that the miller has found at last the peace he sought.

Ex. 7

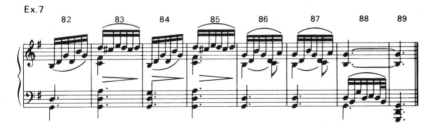

Poetic playing is wanted with special consideration for the penultimate bar where the violoncello-like passage has E for its high point. It is all *pianissimo* and the passing notes on to the tonic chord are treated with loving care.

XX. DES BACHES WIEGENLIED

A STROPHIC song of five verses set in a fairly narrow dynamic range; a rhythmical figure ♩ ♫♩ ♫♩ uniform, monotonous; are these the ingredients of the final song of the cycle? Yes, and monotonous it is. And one would not relinquish one moment of its spell-binding monotony.

No composer other than Schubert can weave such webs of enchantment with such scanty material. As I have already said, who can explain his magic? According to Georges Braque 'In art only one thing counts: that which cannot be explained'. The 'only' is perhaps an exaggeration but in general I go along with this precept, I think of *Wiegenlied* (Seidl's words), *Der liebliche Stern* (Schulze), *Schlaflied* (Mayrhofer), *Die Sterne* (Leitner), all these are related—not poetically but musically —in that their repetitiveness of rhythm, their unsurprising modulations have an hypnotic effect, 'killing care and grief of heart'.

Ex.1

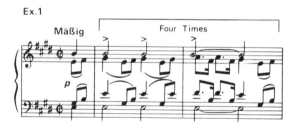

This is the pattern of the entire song, varied somewhat by four bars at 16. Singer and pianist might well ask what *modus operandi* should be adopted to bring some contrast to the even tenor of this music. The answer is that there is little they can or need do about it.

The first two stanzas are devoted to the soothing incantation of the stream as it cradles the drowned lad in its depths: 'tired one you are asleep'.

With *alla breve* as time signature it is significant that almost all the beats throughout are stressed—except where the treble in the accompaniment is tied as in bar 2. In other words first and second beats are

70

given their utmost value. High points during these bars come on the first beats of 2, 4, 6, 8, 10.

In these verses the alto and tenor voices in the accompaniment should be parenthetical, swaying softly and languidly in the current of the stream, sinuous as the long green hair of a naiad.

Apart from the rhythmic stresses there is no need for the singer to sing other than *piano* in this section but at 'Die Treu ist hier' (Faithfulness is here)

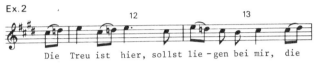

he gives a shade more resonance than before. It is all *molto legato*. At 16 the texture is enriched

'Trinken' bar 17 has an *acciaccatura* or grace note coming before the beat so that the word 'will' is slightly shortened to enable the G sharp to have its full value. The logic of this is seen at 19 where the complementary *appoggiatura* is written out in full.

'The sound of the hunting horn will not be heard in the rush of my waters' and the singer in verse 3 increases his tone to a *mezzoforte* and quickens his pace a little. We now hear more prominently the inner voices of the piano part, reminiscent of the arrogant sound of the horn. At 12 the pianist returns to the original *tempo moderato* preparatory to 'Blue flowers, look not down' (Ex. 2). But at 'ihr macht meinem Schläfer die Traüme so schwer' (you trouble the dreams of my sleeper) the accented chords in the accompaniment are heavy and a sense of restlessness can be conveyed by holding them longer and shortening the following quavers (see Ex. 3). The performers will not distort the rhythm if they carefully avoid exaggeration: the listener must not be allowed to recognize *how* they are achieving this effect of unrest.

'Away, away from the mill-path, light maiden, away, lest your shadow disturb him' (verse 4) gives the singer a chance to make 'Hinweg, hinweg' convincing by cutting short the second syllable thus:

Ex.4

Hin-weg,   hin-weg

It is a plain-spoken dismissal and would be meaningless if sung *legato*.

Finally: 'Good night, good night till the whole world wakes. Sleep out your joy and your sorrow; the full moon rises, the mists are lifting and the heavens above are limitless'.

The singer has been reserving his softest tones for this last verse and he begins 'Gute Nacht, gute Nacht' with infinite tenderness.

It is now that a transcendental grandeur begins to be revealed, born at 12 (Ex. 2). A *crescendo* gathers and grows at 'Der Vollmond steigt' until the climax is reached at 'Der Himmel da oben' 17 (Ex. 3). The singer glories in this passage and it is not unnatural for him to make his top G sharp last a little longer than formerly. 'Der Himmel da oben' is repeated quietly and dies away (19–20) but the *fortepiano* sign, desirable in the earlier verses, should be disregarded; a feeling of peace prevails in this echoing phrase and nothing should disturb it.

With the pianoforte postlude we notice again that repeated note in the treble whose sinister implication first made its impression in *Die liebe Farbe*. Now it becomes a dulcet chime whose tolling lulls the dear lad to his final rest.

> 'His are the quiet steeps of dreamland,
> The waters of no more pain.'

WINTERREISE

I. GUTE NACHT

IN AT least eight songs in this cycle we see the wanderer trudging over the snow becoming increasingly weary in mind and body. Apart from these there are half a dozen songs of quick, even violent movement but they are not, to put it literally, in a 'walking tempo'. The pace in 'Gute Nacht' is more regular than in any other; there is no stumbling, no limping, for the man is only at the beginning of his journey. Even so Schubert did not intend it to be performed with metronomical exactitude, as an examination of his marking tells us. This is not a man marching with military precision, but one with a purpose whose will drives him on, whose resolution impels him to remove himself as far as he may from all that reminds him of his lost love. And yet, bitterness of mind notwithstanding he needs must yield to the ache in his heart to whisper 'Good-night' as he passes the house of the sleeping woman.

Here is a chance for the performers to use poetic imagination, for the composition though strophic, is compounded of painful regret and tender remembrance. The lover leaves the house of the woman who has betrayed him, and in the snow he begins his tortured journey.

'A wanderer I came here, a wanderer I go. May welcomed me with spring blossoms, the maiden talked of love to me and the mother even spoke of marriage. But now the world is gloomy, no trace of a path. I will follow the deer's track with my moon-shadow as companion.'

Though the poor man knows not whither his footsteps are taking him, the performers, aware that this is the longest song in the set and having mapped out their course in advance, know exactly where *they* are going and what they are going to do about it. They firmly understand that the cycle needs a large canvas and is not a series of miniatures; this they make evident at the outset. A strong balance of tone is immediately established: it would be misleading to the listener to begin with the slightest suggestion of tentativeness. The tone should be strong and definite, *mezzo forte*, a level from which the singer can increase his tone —as he will wish to do in the third verse—without going so far as a *fortissimo* and from which he is enabled to diminish to a *pianissimo* without becoming too inaudible in the final stanza.

75

Ex.1

The recommended basic tempo is ♩ = 52, a normal walking pace, and it is firmly established in this introduction. There is a difference between the *forte piano* signs in 2 and 3 and the stress in 4. The latter is a time stress only. These false accents or *tenuti* breaking up the uniformity of the forward movement are expressive of sighs, rather than hesitation in the stride, and should therefore be played as unpercussively as possible.

Ex.2

It is a sweeping line. The high points in these two phrases are marked X, these are more significant than the top notes and the singer thinks of them at the start of each phrase so that he presses on to them with inevitability. A weighty *legato* on the semiquavers is wanted especially in 14 where it presages the sad words 'Das Mädchen sprach von Liebe'. These bars 16–23 are sung *piano* and the singer will be helped if he hears the counter melody in the pianoforte, singing in duo with him.

Ex.3

What can bars 24, 25 with their *forte piano* and > marks mean other than sad sighs?

A little reduction in volume is needed in verse two—as compared with the opening—but again at 15–23 it becomes more *legato* and lyrical.

We are warned that a different mood takes possession by the way the introduction to the third verse is played.

'Why should I tarry longer here until I am driven out? Only dogs howl at their master's door. Love must wander—God has made it so. My darling, Good-night.'

This interlude, a duplication of Example 1, makes a gradual and explicit *crescendo* with a slight quickening of tempo in 38, 39 (these are bars 6, 7 in Ex. 1) to help the singer communicate this mood of angry impatience; it is unmistakably the dynamic apex of the song though of short duration, but Schubert's variation of bars 10 and 14 (Ex. 2) gives the singer every chance to make the most of it:

Ex. 4

After this the pianist makes a sudden *diminuendo* and returns in 47 to the original tempo for 'Die Liebe liebt das Wandern'. Again comes a swift change of mood prepared too by the pianoforte: bitterness now gives way to sadness and we hear it in bars 60 and 64, which, compared with 28 and 31 have so much more heart-burning. Suffering is expressed by the tortured and twice-uttered 'Gute Nacht'.

Ex. 5

It is in the last verse that we come to the moment of truth.

'I'll not disturb your dreams, you will not hear my footsteps as I leave, nor the soft closing of the door. Over the threshold I will write the words "Good-night" that you may know I thought of you.'

It would be better for the lover and his equilibrium if he could depart without so much as a backward glance at her window. Were he able thus to harden his heart there would be no Winter's Journey, no suffering and tears, no storms, no cruel dreams and torturing fantasies: there would be no mental collapse. Alas, he knows with all his soul that he loves her, will never be able to forget her. This is the cycle's raison d'être and why I call this verse the moment of truth. It must be prepared carefully in the interlude by a gradual *diminuendo* with a short pause on the final dominant chord (a hesitant delay but not a break in tone) before we are eased into the major, when *tempo primo* is immediately resumed.

The vocal line is shaped as in the previous verses but is now sung with tenderness; generally it is *pianissimo* though without loss of propulsion.

Ex. 6

Once again the lowest notes are given emphasis on 'nicht stören' and 'nicht hören'—this time most gently. It is a stanza which needs the smoothest singing, yet in two places the *legato* line is broken: at 77, 78 'sacht, sacht' (soft, soft) are separated with very clear enunciation, and at 82 a comma before 'Gute Nacht' will make the words much more expressive. The effect of these breaks in tone is spoiled if breath is taken.

Only on the final 'an dich hab ich gedacht' (I thought of you) comes the authorized *ritardando*. It is a much softer echo of the preceding phrase.

an dich hab ich ge -dacht, an dich hab ich ge - dacht.

The postlude takes up the walking pace at 99 but the phrase 'I thought of you' lingers; we are reminded of it in the inner voices of the pianoforte in 101 and 103.

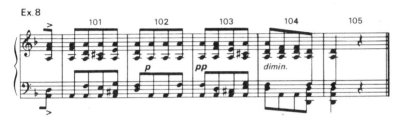

These thoughts, uppermost in the man's mind, are not to be underlined nor brought prominently to one's notice. It is enough that they are there and that the pianist is aware of them.

II. DIE WETTERFAHNE

'THE WIND plays with the weather vane on my Love's house and in my folly I thought it was mocking the poor fugitive. This should have been a warning to me not to expect constancy in that house. The wind plays wantonly over that roof, but beneath though less loudly, it plays with their hearts. What do they care for my grief? Their girl is a wealthy bride.'

The dynamic surges of tone as the fickle wind rises and falls, the mocking trills in the pianoforte, are reflections of the storm of the heart.

I take ♩. = 66 as the approximate tempo (ziemlich geschwind) and we adhere fairly strictly to this save for two climbs made by voice and pianoforte in unison (to which I refer later), and made in the introduction herewith.

Ex.1

Ziemlich geschwind

There is no starting in low gear and getting in top by stages; the pianoforte starts at full speed. I advise the player to sing—in his mind—the first two bars to alert himself, so that the tempo is in his bones and the flame in his heart before he strikes the first note. I have added a hairpin on the semiquaver in 1 and 2 (I am sure Schubert expected a *crescendo*) to make the ensuing *diminuendo* more practicable; it is resilient, squareness avoided, to put anger in those *crescendi*. On the two trills, the first *forte* (not marked by the composer) the second *piano* (marked) the pianist takes time. These trills need some thought to give them shape and meaning.

Ex. 2

Above, in detail, is the shape the writer endeavours to execute these bars, not with unvarying success. The trills begin on the upper note (C).

The singer will be impatient, he will want the final notes of this introduction (which I have described 'short and sharp') out of his way so that there is a momentary silence before he starts.

I alluded earlier to several climbing phrases where a little elasticity is needed, here is one of them.

Ex.3

Der Wind spielt mit der Wet-terfah-ne auf mei-nes schö-nen Liebchens Haus.

We should feel the tempo pressing on up to 'schönen' where it gives way to the pull back at 'Liebchens Haus'. The phrase is repeated 25–28 and though now marked 'lightly' is shaped in similar fashion. Inconstancy of rhythm in these instances, though slight, contributes to the prevailing turbulence: it would be far easier for the ensemble between the partners if these wind-swept passages were treated in strict time, but the risk then is that they might sound pedestrian. With two minds thinking as one singing and playing as one man—the effect of tempo *rubato* is exciting.

It is hardly possible to exaggerate the precipitous contrasts between *forte* and *piano* in these violent two pages of music. Bars 9–10 in the pianoforte are typical

Ex.4

The three semiquavers surge to a *forte* and without a moment's waiting on the first beat of 10, drop steeply to a *piano*: these dynamic extremes are contained in the space of three seconds. This is played in strict time and it is advisable to keep the tempo steady until we come to 25 (parallel to Ex. 3) for it will enable the singer to barb the words 'sie pfiff'den armen Flüchtling aus' with ironic self-mockery. This bitterness is expressed again in the accompaniment's stinging lashes to the lover's 'never seek a faithful woman in that place'.

Ex.5

hätt er nim - mer su - chen wol-len im Haus ein treu-es Frau-en-bild.

A tight hold on the rhythm is implied by the stresses in 19, 20. It is a control to be exercised at 30 'Was fragen sie nach meinen Schmerzen' (What do they care for my grief?)

Ex. 6

Was fra-gen sie nach mei-nen Schmerzen?

Schubert has written *laut* (noisy) over these words—they are uttered three times—showing what importance the composer attached to them —and are most certainly to be sung *non-legato* with forcible emphasis on each semiquaver. They ascend in the singer's final bars through the keys of F, G minor and A in a storming *crescendo*.

The contrast between these febrile passages and 'The wind plays with their hearts' marked *leise* (low not loud) is explicit.

Throughout the song the pianist must observe the numerous detached chords, but he uses the sustaining pedal on all trills and whenever the wind is howling, the *pianissimo* 35, 36 for instance and the sweeping 45, 46.

Ex. 7

The difference between the postlude and the introduction is to be seen in the rests in 47, 48. They are important, the short silences lend extra energy to the semiquavers that follow. The stresses too seem to demand more sinew in the rhythm.

In nearly every edition there are *appogiaturi* in 15, 16 and they are executed as follows.

Ex. 8

hätt es e-her be - mer -ken sol-len

III. GEFRORNE TRÄNEN

ALTHOUGH THE stride is more laboured in *Gefrorne Tränen* (Frozen Tears) than in *Gute Nacht*, the metronomic speed here is about $\lessdot = 48$, not so far removed from the other's $\lessdot = 52$, but there all affinity between the two songs ends. I mention this because the theory, sometimes expressed, that the pace of one walking song should be the pace for all is a misconception, for fatigue increases the further the wanderer goes, his footsteps become more and more unsteady, his pace naturally slacker.

No other song in the set seems to convey such an impression of biting cold, except the first page of *Auf dem Flusse*. The flesh cringes and the blood congeals with those spiky detached chords in the pianoforte, with those false accents which suggest a shudder rather than a falter in the stride.

The lachrymose plaint of the singer is all the more telling over the *non-legato* accompaniment, if it is delivered with a firm stream of sound. This seems a contradiction but the gnawing disquiet lies in the pianoforte and it is for the singer to tell us what it is all about: the steady tone of the singer is the essence of the song. The voice seems to be unsupported by the pianoforte (although the contrary is the case) and this adds to the desolation of the picture.

'My tears fall frozen from my cheeks. Can I have wept without knowing it? O tears, you turn to ice as easily as the cool dew of morning, yet you spring from a heart whose fire would melt a world of ice.'

Ex.1

The tempo is strict and every mark is vital, especially the *fortepiano* in 3 which makes possible the *decrescendo* in 4. At 7 the *pianissimo* applies to the pianoforte rather than to the voice. Indeed the singer should not be secretive; he needs no less than a *mezzo piano* for his entry and from this he is enabled to make the same *diminuendo* heard in the introduction and to imitate it.

Ex. 2

At 12 comes an over-all *decrescendo* carried on to the *pianissimo* at 21. This indeed is a *pianissimo* and much more so than at 8.

Ex. 3

The *appoggiatura* D flat on 'Tränen' is generally sung as a full crotchet as I have marked in parenthesis.

'O tears, you turn to ice' etc., lies low in the voice and the pianist with consideration plays more softly than anywhere else in the song.

Now the performers think about two approaching high points; the first at 38 and a still greater one at 48.

The *crescendo* at 29 induces the singer to raise his voice but he remembers to hold something in hand for the summit at 38. This is big indeed and the sibilant consonants of 'des ganzen Winters Eis' are as the hissing of the wind in our ears.

Throughout this progressive build-up of tone the pianoforte's stresses—particularly those off the beat—are becoming more and more prominent until at 35, 36, 37 marked *sforzando*, they are ponderous (a

Ex.4

heavy foot crunching the ice in the frozen cart track). The pianist falls onto the stressed minim in these bars; after the first beat he delays his drop on to these *sforzandi* to make them more cogent.

I would draw the pianist's attention to the tenor voice in his accompaniment at 33 and 43 where it echoes the vocal line.

With the final 'des ganzes Winters Eis' the singer at last reaches his *fortissimo* and he holds the last note unrelentingly as marked, with no weakening of tone.

Ex.5

The postlude sinks lower and lower in pitch and in volume, never losing its dryness. Nor should it slow down; we should finish the song without a stereotyped *rallentando*. The walker is not tarrying, he is going on and we strengthen this idea by keeping to the iron rhythm. Only our dynamics, as the tone becomes softer and softer, warn us we are arriving at the closing cadence; this, and a fractional pause or comma before the final tonic chord.

IV. ERSTARRUNG

THE ORIGINAL instruction for this song was 'Nicht zu geschwind' (not too quick) subsequently amended to 'Ziemlich geschwind' (rather quick): one dissuasive and the other suasive. There is certainly a distinction between the two and I feel the last urges more speed than the first. At a tempo of $\downarrow = 152$ the song takes just under three minutes to perform.

Schubert flung himself on these verses with fever heat. He could not write the notes down fast enough, which accounts, perhaps, for his revision of the tempo and also for his mistaking 'erstorben' (dead) for 'erfroren' (frozen) in bar 83. The mistake, seen in many editions, is ascribed by Richard Capell to the composer's haste, and the singer would be well advised to heed this eminent Schubertian when he says 'erstorben' (83) upsets the sense. Müller wrote 'die Blumen sind erstorben' followed by 'Mein Herz ist wie erfroren' and it should be sung this way.

Sometimes, in order to fill out or embellish his design, to give more emphasis to a mood or to paint more vividly a scene, Schubert would repeat a musical phrase. He does it in the previous songs, *Die Wetter-fahne* and *Gefrorne Tränen*. In *Erstarrung* he has recourse to this process of 'filling out' more than in any other song in the cycle: there are five quatrains and each one is repeated. The structure for each repeated stanza, its merging with the next—its inevitable and gradual ascent to the final climax—combine to make this song something of an architectural marvel.

The distracted man searches in the snow for the footprints of his beloved. He walked with her, arm in arm, when these fields were green. His tears will melt the ice and snow that he may see and kiss the earth beneath.

Schubert could easily have written the first eight bars of the vocal line as follows:

Ex.1

Did I say easily? Well it would have been the line of least resistance but would not have satisfied Schubert when he was on fire. Compare bars 12 to 15 above with this:

Ex.2

and now the entire verse is repeated but not to the ready-made notation seen above:

Ex.3

Even without the pianoforte to support it, this melodic line is a composition in itself: it is instinct with painful agitation; it climbs gradually up to the high point 'meine Arme' (13) then sinks to 'grüne Flur' (23) without ever losing its motive power.

There is a *pianissimo* sign at 8 but the singer will need more tone to carry over the accompaniment.

Never is there a moment in the song, never a beat when the pianoforte is not playing triplets, they are either in the treble or bass; and in the third verse both hands are busy with them.

As in *Die Wetterfahne* the player is 'in the tempo' before he begins his introduction so that we are plunged immediately into the appointed speed.

Ex.4

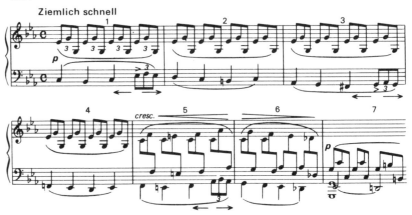

The right hand, supplying the ferment, is felt rather than heard: it is not unimportant—every note should be there—but in the first stanza the left hand predominates. Those sinister shuddering triplets in the bass (1, 3, 5) are a feature of the song and must be considered. They are obviously to be emphasized without being made to stand out disproportionately. By delaying the fourth beat (that is, holding back the triplets' entry), one is impelled to hurry it and this gives an effect of restlessness and irregularity. The right hand goes on its way imperviously—it is for the left hand to catch up. I have tried in the example above to indicate my meaning. These bass triplets fall without exception on the fourth beat of the bar.

'I will kiss the earth' in the second verse sees a thrilling argument between the voice and the pianoforte's treble: these two lines cross and re-cross each attacking and retreating, rising and falling in turn.

Ex.5

'Tränen', bar 30, is the high point rather than 'meinen heissen' and time must be allowed for the consonants 'Tr', not only for enunciation's sake but for the drama of it. There is no necessity to arrest the impetus, for these consonants are heard *before* the bar line, they rob the last syllable of 'heissen'.

The repetition of the words is again cast on a higher level (bar 35 etc), and follows the design of the first verse.

After the hectic impetuosity of the first two verses, we now hear the pitiful cry 'Where shall I find a flower, where green grass? The flowers are dead, the turf is bare'. As colour and pattern of the writing change so we see for the first time since bar 8 *pianissimo* on the score.

Once again by the interlude, the pianoforte prepares us for this expression of yearning.

Before the new section at 47 the two partners should discuss the handling of bar 46. There is a choice; either to go direct into 47 without the slightest slackening of speed; or to prepare for the change, by giving the two *pizzicato* E flats in the bass a little more time. Though it is not marked, I prefer the second alternative for it is tenderer in feeling, it presages the mood and it is not so matter of fact.

Schubert's marking *legato*, the first time this sign has appeared, implies that the composer expected the singing previous to this to have been declamatory. Now it is unlaboured and less agitated, as the poor man's scurrying in the snow ceases for a space and he abandons himself to these despairing thoughts.

In the example above 'Wo find ich' bars 48 and 50 are the high points but in Ex. 7 they are 'Blüte' and 'Gras'; differences that should be made evident.

The pianoforte whose clearly articulated triplets have contributed so much to the agitation has now become smoother, the sustaining pedal being used more generously than before. Under the eloquent melodic line the accompaniment is subdued.

Schubert does not repeat this verse as it stands. The last half of the quatrain and the first half are transposed so that we have

Ex.7

leading back to the main subject. This is a stroke of conspicuous mastery; confusion of mind is shown by one question tumbling over another. First we had 'Where the flowers, where the grass?' and hard upon these comes 'Is there no memory I can take from here? Is there nothing to remind me of her, save my grief?' The forsaken man finally reaches the sombre conclusion that her picture is frozen in his heart: once this ice melts the vision of her will thaw and disappear with it.

If there has been any tendency to lose speed—and for the sake of expressiveness this will be acceptable if not made too apparent—it should now be regained by an *accelerando* at 64. Thus the procedure at 46, where a slight *rallentando* was made, is reversed, At 65 the tempo must be in full flow.

The form is *a b c a b* therefore verses 4 and 5 are substantially the same as the first two. Now, however, more passion is wanted; the rising passages with their swelling of tone, the descents with their diminution are made more pronounced, we find a *fortissimo* at 97. Also for the first time *un poco ritardando* is seen in the singer's final bar.

It is imperative for the tempo to be resumed in the pianoforte at 103. The bass line sinks down with a long *diminuendo* to the low C, a *pianissimo* which must not be inaudible. The triplets in the treble remain agitated, never becoming slower: only, and in order to give notice of finality, is there a short wait before the last chord. This can best be explained by imagining 108 to be a bar in 5/4 time.

Ex. 8

V. DER LINDENBAUM

'BY THE gates of the little town stands a lime tree, under its shade I enjoyed many a day-dream. I carved loving words on its bark. In happiness and in sorrow I felt it call me to its sheltering branches.'

It has been said more than once in these pages that the player must be 'in the tempo' before he starts to play, but in this introduction that ukase does not apply.

Ex. 1

The chord of E major should be well established and fall soothingly on the ear; impatience to leave it robs it of all relaxation. Let us stay for a moment on the G sharp and as we make the slight increase in tone we simultaneously quicken the tempo to the top of the hairpin; on the descent with its *diminuendo* we correspondingly retard. Rise and fall are only from *pp* to *p* and back: these delicate traceries in the treble are no more than the rustling of leaves on a still night.

In the above example the longest bars are 2, 7, and 8: especially bar 2 where the minim is held to its fullest extent. (Not so easy as it sounds, for the pianist—nervous at performance—anxious to get to grips with his quivering semiquaver passage—is apt to relinquish that sustained note too soon. It needs control, but by exercising it the player puts the listener at his ease.) The answering long B in the bass (4) must be clear. Points of rest are 7 with its echo at 8.

Ease? Relaxation? Yes, the wanderer sees in his imagination this tree with verdure clad, he transports us back to summer days: for a transient moment he feels no cold, is unaware of snow.

Ex. 2

The first verse is not sung in a hushed voice, it is *piano* of course, but the singer is inspired by happy recollection rather than regret, his tone is lyrical and light.

We find several rests where it would seem the flow of the sentence would be interrupted by breathing; bars 10, 14, 22 are instances, and the rests must be observed, but are the breaths necessary? To some singers they are not, but I believe Schubert gave the singer these moments for breathing to prevent any sense of effort, so that repose would be undisturbed. Between 'Tore' and 'da' there is no need at all for any movement of the lips in order to take in air and it is easily done with the listener none the wiser.

The quavers in 9 move forward to 'Tore'; bar 11 is a little longer for the triplets on 'Lindenbaum' are affectionately unhurried; 'ich traümt' and 'ich schnitt' are allowed time too, with expressive enunciation on the consonants—consonants it would be a shame to hasten. Yet the movement is never allowed to sink back on its heels; this is the singer's responsibility and he will be helped if the pianoforte moves with utmost lightness.

By a change to the minor the man is brought back to the gloomy picture of the present.

'On my journey I passed my tree at night and although it was dark I closed my eyes. Yet its branches seemed to murmur "Come friend, here you will find peace".'

The rustling motif is heard again in the interlude but the enchantment of the major key has gone, it is now heavy-hearted and the tempo
—with intentional absence of freshness—a trifle slower. The *pianissimo*
mark of the introduction is missing, suggesting the need for more
sonority: this applies particularly to the stressed notes on 26 and 28
(again held) with 28 the more portentous—its two bass notes played
with deliberation.

Ex. 3

With resolution the singer regains the tempo as if he were shaking
off almost impatiently the futile visions of summer, a feeling reinforced
by the triplets' urge in the pianoforte and the accents in 29, 30.

Even so the poor man is easily persuaded that the murmuring
branches are saying 'hier findst du deine Ruh' and we are taken back to
the major key.

But!

Ex. 4

An icy gust, a flurry of snow rudely bring the lonely man down to earth.

'The cold wind beats my face, blows my hat off, but I'll not turn back.'

The silence in 44—in other words the quaver rest—is pregnant and should be slightly prolonged. Thus the *sforzando* in 45 is made more shattering.

Everything depends on the pianist in the next dozen bars: howling wind, the reeling figure (46, 48) are depicted in his part. Pedal must be used in plenty and sensitive attention paid to the singer at 52, 53 so that his low notes are not smothered.

Ex. 5

Again the wind blusters momentarily, then dies away as the interlude takes us into the last verse.

'Many hours of tramping have taken me far from that spot yet still the lime tree calls "Here is peace".'

Ex. 6

This is sung, if possible, even more tenderly and nostalgically than before. The singer gives the pianist time for his tones to clear, then a moment's hush, a slight *tenuto* on his up-beat 'Nun', and once again we hear that enchanting tune. It is sung *pianissimo* with the emotional high point 'Du fändest Ruhe dort' whispered with an intimate intensity.

The accompanying triplet figure should have none of the urgency it had in the minor section; now it is consolatory, and it retires below the tonal level of the voice. Those little quavers in the bass, marked *staccato* I prefer to regard as *pizzicato* for they are played gently with a touch of the sustaining pedal and are a long way removed from the dry, shrivelled *staccato* we wanted in *Gefrorne Tränen*.

As if the singer could not bear to lose these magical moments the words are repeated with rising emotion.

The rhythmical notation met at bar 43 (Ex. 4) is varied at bar 75 and the singer lingers on the last note of his triplet with consideration so that the pianoforte semiquaver is played without haste.

One must add that of all *The Winter's Journey* this song is the one to be plucked most frequently out of the cycle and sung in a miscellaneous group of Schubert Lieder.

When Schubert sang and played these twenty four songs for the first time to a circle of intimate friends, *Der Lindenbaum* was the only one they liked, they were perplexed and downcast by the gloom of the rest.

Der Lindenbaum with its lovely melody, its dreaming, its moments of 'Sturm und Drang', its picturesque suggestions in the pianoforte, is perhaps more perceptible at first hearing than its fellows, but to imagine thereby that it excels the others betrays but a superficial acquaintance with the remaining twenty-three songs.

VI. WASSERFLUTH

THE QUESTION of the bass semiquaver coming with or after the treble triplet was raised in the chapter on *Ungeduld* (*Die Schöne Müllerin*) and readers will be aware I am in full agreement with Desmond Shawe-Taylor when he said that the semiquaver lagging behind (as it appears on the score) symbolizes the tired laboured footsteps of the wanderer. If we are opposed to this view the introduction will look like this:

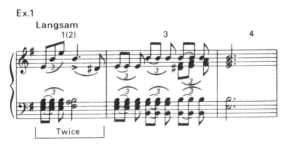

To be consistent bar 3 is symmetrical and in consequence loses character and gives no suggestion of struggle.

I am convinced it should be played *as it looks* on the score.

This has meaning.

We see above, a rhythmical figure that is reminiscent of the accompaniment to the last verse of *Der Lindenbaum* (Ex. 6). There is a resemblance but that is all, for here the texture is heavier, the tempo slower and the mood lugubrious. A tendency to make the D sharp in 1 and 2 a triplet must be watched; this note comes on the half beat.

'My tears drop into the snow. A warm breeze will melt the snow and it will flow away bearing my tears with it. Snow, you know of my longing and the stream will take you through the town. Then, when you feel my teardrops burning you will surely know—there is my darling's house.'

Capell sums it up as a torrent of tears that will be released by the spring thaw. It is indeed an extravagant fancy but the nobility of the vocal line with its sweeping phrases more than restores credibility. A slight comma or lift up after the last chord of the introduction (and interludes) helps to make the singer's attack more incisive.

Ex.3

A *legato* line is at once established by the singer—not for him a *pianissimo* as in the pianoforte—for he offsets the sentimentality of the words by the firmness of his tone. Spells of weakness on the pilgrim's part frequently occur in these songs and if, as in *Wasserfluth*, they are unfolded too tremulously they effeminize the man. Spacious rises and falls in pitch and volume come later but here in the first six bars (5–10) a level tone is kept. Taut rhythm on 7 is important, the dotted quavers and short semiquavers markedly different from the triplets.

At 11 and 12 comes the first of our big *crescendi* up to 'heisse Weh'.

Ex.4

Schubert's instructions on 'Weh' require examination. Obviously the high point dramatically is the F natural, yet this note is delayed so that the agonized discord of the pianoforte's F clashes with the singer's E. This discord must be well and truly heard. When the singer reaches the summit of his climb he finds his F is given short shrift, for a *diminuendo* follows at once. Is the minor third drop to be sung without semblance of a *portamento*? No, its use here is vital—it is a heart-rending sigh. I do not advocate a slide from one note to another with recklessness but the truth is that the *portamento* is a wonderfully effective weapon in the singer's armoury provided he uses it sparingly and provided he uses it with intent. When the singer is unaware he is sliding from one note to another he has become an addict. This is unbearable.

The two climaxes come at the end of each verse

As the singer's tone ceases at 28 on the clearly enunciated T of 'zerrinnt' the pianoforte's tone stops too; both artists release their note at exactly the same moment. There is an appreciable and dramatic silence before the interlude begins at 29.

The same procedure is followed at 56 but with more intensity. This outburst is preceded by the softest phrases in the song.

My term 'softest' hardly describes the quality of voice demanded for 'You will feel my tears burning, and will know—there is my darling's house'. All this is indeed *pianissimo* but is sung as though the poor man were holding on to himself with all his strength for fear of collapsing, it is sung as if through clenched teeth.

Bars 55, 56 are similar to 27, 28 but far outweigh them and are more frenzied. On 'Haus' the tone swells and swells up to the explosion on the final 'S' whose sibilance is purposely exaggerated. Again the pianist's tone stops abruptly with the voice. He prolongs the solemn stillness before quietly bringing the song to a conclusion.

Wasserfluth was originally written in F sharp minor, its *tessitura* embraced top A's and G sharps; this is in the tenor range and an uncomfortable altitude for a baritone. The cycle does call for the deeper and darker quality of a baritone as opposed to a bright tenor and Schubert, on second thoughts and perhaps advised by Michael Vogl, transposed the song to a lower key, more conformable to the baritone range and more in keeping with the colour of the other songs in the set.

Likewise *Rast, Einsamkeit, Muth* and *Der Leiermann* were later transposed down.

VII. AUF DEM FLUSSE

MOVING AT a funereal pace the wayfarer reflects how the clear running river that once sparkled so happily now appears motionless under its coating of ice. On the hard crust he carves with a flint the name of his love and the dates of their first meeting and his farewell; a broken ring encircles it all. 'My heart' he asks, 'do you not see your own image in this frozen stream? Is there not a raging torrent beneath this icy surface?'

Ex.1

What could look more uneventful than this introduction? It has a deceptive simplicity, for the player will find it necessary to practise it over and over again to achieve the effect he wants. The *staccato* cannot be exaggerated—it is even more *staccato* than *Gefrorne Tränen*—the notes are veritable pin-pricks of sound. Starting from *ppp* we *crescendo* at 2 up to a *pp* at 3 and then retreat to a *ppp*. Nothing could be more microscopic than this undulation of tone. Of course no sustaining pedal is used. These four bars are fascinating to the pianist and demand

sensitive ears and mind. The song is as numbed with cold for the first
twenty bars as *Gefrorne Tränen*.

Beautiful though the German language can be it is so profuse with
consonants that it is impossible to keep a *legato* vocal line and at the
same time enunciate the words clearly. Of course the words can be
sacrificed, but that is an alternative to be avoided. A consummate
artist deceives the listener: when he sings 'so lustig rauschtest' with its
important onomatopoeia, so intense is his delivery, so expert his timing
of the consonants that it is not noticed that the singing sound along
with the vowels has been momentarily lost.

Ex.2

Der du so lu - stig rauschtest, du hel - ler, wil - der Fluß,

'So lustig rauschtest' is made crystal clear and keeps to the pulse beat
of the introduction. As I say, it is *legato* as far as it is possible to make
it.

At 8 the up beat 'wie' is held, preparing us for the ensuing drop in
tone and *making room* for the consonants of 'still', for the 's' poaches
on the territory of 'wie'.

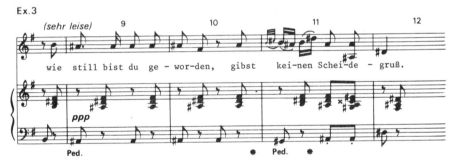

Ex.3

(sehr leise)

wie still bist du ge - wor-den, gibst kei-nen Schei-de - gruß.

ppp

Ped.   * Ped. *

This preparation is made for the cutting modulation to D sharp
minor, a resolution signalized in the pianoforte by the use—for the
first time—of the sustaining pedal. It is an arresting moment which the
composer had in view with his 'sehr leise'.

I cannot emphasize too strongly how vital it is for the pianist to be as
sparing as possible with the sustaining pedal, especially in songs where
Schubert has marked *staccato*. He wants the playing to be *sec* when his
theme is the scene with its icy coldness. The *legato* line of the voice
stands out in relief against this dry colour nor is the singer's *sotto voce*

in danger of being covered. But judiciously used, as we see in Ex. 3, the pedal adds varieties of colours to the pianist's palette. It brings feeling and illumination. Here too, it gives inspiration to the singer when he refers to 'the name of my darling' in the following example.

Ex.4

This page of the score in E major is in two eight-bar sections, the second part being a varied repetition of the first, varied because the heart beats quicken at the carving of her name (that fluttering accompaniment) and because the 'broken ring' is a piercing thought.

Was ever 'sob' written more convincingly than that 'zerbrockner Ring'? Schubert has sobbed himself with the drop of the sixth and the despairing inflexion up to 'Ring'. The singer would bring shame on himself and embarrassment to his hearers if he attempted to gild the lily by

Ex.5

singing the phrase with an operatic sob. I repeat, Schubert has done it.

One breath suffices for the above, and if the singer is nearing the end of his tether at 38 it makes no matter. The pianist supports the voice with his pedal in these moments, but once he embarks on his interlude at 38, bleakness again obtains.

There is no 'by your leave' about the silence in 40, it interrupts abruptly; also its elongation is a dramatic stepping-stone to a duo between the voice and the pianoforte's bass wherein the man compares the river's movement below its still surface to the agitation in his own heart. 'Der du so lustig rauschtest' sings the accompaniment and the singer feels this underneath him and embellishes it with his own fantasy. The tempo and weight are exactly the same as at the song's beginning, though the tortured 'erkennst du nun dein Bild' is almost whispered.

At 48 comes our first *forte*, suddenly, as if the angry waters shake off the shackling ice with a mighty heave.

The singer startles us. His tone is resounding and he allows no tailing off at the end of his phrases, even the 'schwilt' at 54 is aggressively *forte* to the accompaniment's *subito pianissimo*; all the same he does not dwell long on this note out of consideration for the motif in the pianoforte. Apart from the exceptional 'schwilt' the bass in the pianoforte is given equal volume with the voice, and the player drops onto his *staccato* D sharp in 49 with the heavy deliberation he showed in a similar situation in *Gefrorne Tränen* (the D flats in Ex. 4 of that song). His treble now is noisy and the demisemiquavers are dashed off angrily.

It would be inaccurate to state that bars 41 to 54 are repeated. The words are the same, the design the same, but we are taken now to F sharp minor, to G minor, before returning to the home key: as the pianist delves deeper into the bass, the singer is given higher summits to scale.

Although this is the singer's last phrase, I feel a *rallentando* would be too commonplace; none the less it would be a shame to stick too strictly to tempo in this crowning passage. On the other hand if the singer skids too hastily off his top A, his listeners will suspect he is afraid of it. The solution—I confess it looks ghastly on paper—is to give the top A an extra semiquaver and make no other slowing up at all. The postlude dies away to nothing with the last chord spread very deliberately.

In Ex. 7 the alternative passage can be seen. The composer was aware of course that the high notes might be beyond the normal baritone range but with respect, I feel that this substitution is very lack-lustre beside the original. This song and *Wasserfluth* lose nothing by being transposed down one tone, the latter into E minor and *Auf dem Flusse* to D minor.

VIII. RÜCKBLICK

'Though I am tramping over ice and snow my feet are burning. I cannot pause to take breath until that town is out of sight. Every stone seems to make me stumble, even the crows scrape snow over me from the housetops as I labour to get away.'

The desperate man has not yet put the town behind him. I like to think he has taken a short cut through some narrow alley where his voice reverberates from wall to wall. This fancy is bred by the extra-ordinary effect of the singer's melodic line being pursued in canon-style and mocking echo by the pianoforte—now in the bass, now in the alto voice. Together this conflict produces a reverberation likely to occur in a passage or alley between houses. (That he is in a narrow confine also explains his apparent inability to avoid the crows' missiles.)

Ex.1

A speed of ♩ = 112 is not at odds with Schubert's instructions. There are several reasons why a quicker tempo is impracticable: the singer has many words to articulate and they will be extremely difficult to enunciate clearly and therefore unintelligible to the listener; also, voice and pianoforte tumbling over one another in such grand confliction develop into a grand muddle. Rhythmic control must be exercised.

So in this example bars 1, 3, 5, 7 (each with its rumbling *crescendo* from a *piano* to a *forte*) are speeded up to the *sf*, and on 2, 4, 6, the movement is held back during the *diminuendo*, the high point being the *fp* on 6. It will be seen that the even-numbered bars are *piano* but bar 8 breaks this pattern by calling attention to itself with an angry *forte*: 9 and 10 are echoes of the two preceding bars. The same pedal is held through the chromatic climb wherever it occurs.

Ex.2

No fluctuations of tempo, as I suggested for the introduction, are made by the singer in the first section of the song. He presses on fiercely, each note is pointed and the words tumble over one another with vigorous projection. Under the circumstances a *legato* line, such as he found it possible to achieve in the quick moving *Erstarrung*, is not to be expected. But the singer should not infer that each note is necessarily detached, he always bears in mind the build up of the *crescendo* to 'Eis und Schnee' in 13, to 'Türme seh' in 16. If his mind is reaching out for these high points before he makes his *crescendo*, he obviates the impression of *staccato*.

The pianoforte bass and alto voices imitate the singer's dynamics as exactly as possible, clattering brashly on the *forte* marks.

My interpretation of Schubert's sign > as a time stress must be unashamedly discarded at 21 and at its counterpart 24.

The pleasing pain of recalling the past is expressed by a new subject. Its mood, although there is no musical resemblance, is a reminder of *Der Lindenbaum* with the jilted man looking back to days when hopes were high and love returned. This change is announced in the interlude's soothing *rallentando* as it moves into the major key, and by the *fermata* in 27, where the wayfarer pauses to take breath.

Ex.4

'How differently you first welcomed me, fickle town. The lark and nightingale sang at your bright windows, the lime trees were in bloom and the fountains gushed. Two eyes shone lovingly on you and then, poor fellow, you were lost.'

Angry determination turns, as we see, to tenderness, a smooth lyrical line succeeds vigorous declamation. Even 'Unbeständigkeit' (inconstancy) is sung regretfully and not resentfully and should be shaped with grace.

All through these two quiet verses with their undulating line, the singer's sights are set on the high point 'und ach, zwei Mädchenaugen glühten' an emotive phrase repeated with increased fervour.

Rustling leaves and the flash of water are softly pictured in the pianoforte treble, but it will be seen at 40, 41, that the accompaniment is constructed to give added support to the voice's climb.

Although it forsakes its rippling broken octave movement it is not to be confused with the crabbed temper of the introduction but played as unpercussively as can be and with sustaining pedal.

These two verses unlike the rest should be *molto tranquillo* and are to be performed at a more relaxed tempo than ♩ = 112; they stand out in pronounced contrast from the others.

But at 47, 48 comes the link between this fragmentary calm and the passionate longing of the finale.

The major in 47 holds to the calm mood, but at 48 immediately the minor chord sounds (not on the first beat) the pianist accelerates and has regained *tempo primo* for the voice's entry.

'When thoughts of those days come to me, I long to look back, to return, to stand mute before her house.'

Again, as in the last stanza of *Gute Nacht* the poor man is faced with the truth: trudge on as he will, his heart and his mind are behind in that accursed town.

Even though the sonority in the last stanza is reduced, the flame burns no less fiercely than at the song's beginning. The passionate yearning is heard in 55 and 57 with slight *tenuti* on 'Tag' and 'einmal', a clinging to those notes to underline the hopelessness of it all. 'Zurükke' and 'wanken' are similarly held and these Schubert has marked (59–60).

Ex. 7

kömmt mir der Tag in die Ge - danken, möcht ich noch einmal rückwärts sehn

A gentle *ritenuto* on the forlorn triplets in 66 brings the song to an end.

Ex. 8

vor ih-rem Hau-se stil - le stehn.

In some editions the penultimate bar is printed with the treble and bass chords being played simultaneously, but the above is authentic.

IX. IRRLICHT

AT LONG last our wayfarer, torn from out the town, finds himself in a strange region. He has been following a will o' the wisp along the frozen bed of a stream into a rock-bound gully. It seems to be a maze. How he will find his way out does not trouble him so used is he by now to aimless rambling. 'Joy and sorrow are the playthings of this capricious lure' he says, 'I will follow this stream's dry course for it will lead to the sea as surely as sorrow leads to the grave'.

The vocal line is picturesque with an extensive range and an imposing carriage. Judging by his very first utterance the singer seems more impressed by 'die tiefsten Felsengründe' than by the fascination of the lure; this perhaps is understandable in one who says 'Bin gewohnt das Irregehen' (I am used to straying).

Bars 5 and 6 are delivered with a full tone, it would belie the qualifying 'tiefsten' were 'Felsengründe' to be lightened. For all his absorption in the scenery, I feel that the 32nd notes (or demisemiquavers) with their skittish rhythm are reminders of this will o' the wisp, and the distinction between them and the semiquavers must be made plain; the singer therefore, without disturbing the steady pulse beat, stays as long as he dare on 'In' (5) and on the first syllables of 'Felsengründe' and 'lockte' (6, 7) and of course on 'mich'. To do this and still make his words clear is not easy but, nevertheless, he should follow this practice at all times in the song.

It is typical of Schubert that this jerking, angular shape reduces in no wise the solemnity of the music.

The pianoforte is concerned with the decoy. It is heard in the introduction (3, 4) and in nearly every bar accompanying the voice. We see it
in bar 7 where the marking is explicit. To make the soprano voice
staccato the sustaining pedal cannot be used; the lower voices, *non
staccato*, are played with an organist's touch—the fingers crawling over
the keys. (In some editions the third beat in bars 3, 7, 19 is not marked
staccato but this is an omission not in accordance with Mandyczewski).
Against the voice's firm line this mocking *staccato*, typifying the ghostly
twinkling 'Irrlicht', shows up in eerie contrast. In 9 and 10 the hands
are almost chucked onto the keyboard to give those short notes the
skittishness they need.

It is scarcely necessary for me to add that the third beat of 13 under
the singer's triplet is treated by the pianist in exactly the same rhythm
as the third beat of 11.

Except for slight variations in the vocal line, the second verse is a
repetition of the first.

Ex. 2

Bin ge-wohnt das Ir - re - ge - hen, 's führt ja je - der Weg   zum

Ziel: un-sre Freu den, uns-re We - hen,

My principal reason for giving this illustration is to draw attention
to 'unsre Wehen' in 22. It does rhyme, after all, with 'Irregehen' in
18 and this is how Müller wrote it. Admittedly it is almost automatic
to say 'Freuden und Leiden' and it is frequently printed and sung this
way. The mistake—for it appears in the original manuscript—must be
ascribed once again to Schubert's haste. It shows, and not for the first
time, that our divinely inspired Franz was, when all is said and done, a
human being, and we love him for it.

No illusion is made to the will o' the wisp in the final stanza and as a
consequence the music is even more majestic than before. We are
reminded of the barren surroundings by the dissonances in the pianoforte,   Ex. 3

but in 33 and 37 the singer must not be circumscribed by the bar lines
in his glorious sweeping phrases, his 32nd notes are not hurried and,
above all he dwells—for a small space only—on the high G's.

None of the expression marks in Ex. 4 are other than Mandyczewski,
and it will be observed that the all embracing *fermata* (to be seen
in Schubert's manuscript) over the last four notes in 39 indicates
that the bar is a timeless one, sung as a recitative, *a piacere*. It is an
expressive and taxing phrase for the singer and has to be contained in
one breath. The intrusive consonants between G and F sharp (ch and
s) are deliberate and the consonants in 'Grab' even more so. If the singer
invests the words with meaning and without making us aware of the
technical feat involved, the whole phrase is made very moving.

Perhaps some explanation of my feeling about this song, by way of
summing up, is desirable.

We find in *Irrlicht* for the first time in the cycle no direct or oblique
reference to the jilt who has broken the man's heart. Pain is still there,
but it is subjugated; there are no tears, no self-pity, no spleen. The man
looks at himself and his situation with a philosophical detachment and
gains thereby in dignity. This is why I feel it should be delivered in a
strong manly way, with the voice impervious to the waywardness of
the pianoforte. It is the reason too for my description of the vocal line
in such terms as 'imposing' and 'majestic'.

For a baritone, B minor is an extremely high key. It does no harm to
the song to sing it in A minor and there are printed editions in that key.

In Ex. 1 and 4 the *appoggiaturi* are taken thus:

X. RAST

Rast was conceived in the key of D minor but on the original manuscript in Schubert's own hand are written the words 'Auch in C moll'. We are grateful for the consideration and are taking advantage of this indulgence by discussing the song in the lower key.

It is only as he lies down to rest that the wanderer realizes how exhausted he is. 'It was too cold to tarry on the road and the storm drove me on, my feet needed no rest, my back felt no burden.'

The introduction wearily drags one foot after the other. By his stresses on the second beats, by his *staccato* on each quaver in the bass the composer, short of writing the actual word '*rubato*' (a term he never used even if he were acquainted with it) is surely indicating that some empathy is needed. The performers ask themselves how they would walk if they were dog-tired. Would each stride be of equal length, each footfall uniform? It is a stumbling gait, an almost unnoticed departure from regularity which, if exaggerated becomes ludicrous: the pianist must be on his guard. It is the kind of passage one never plays twice in exactly the same way. Of only one thing can you be certain; a *rallentando* towards the end must be made and a long pause on bar 6 as if to lean against a tree trunk to recover your breath.

Ex.1

The singer, in no hurry, waits for the last chord to clear before his entry.

Ex.2

Nun merk ich erst, wie müd ich bin, da ich zur Ruh mich le - ge;

das Wan-dern hielt mich mun-ter hin auf un-wirt ba-rem We - ge.

Paradoxically the singer makes a mistake by taking advantage of each comma in the text to chop the music into short phrases simulating breathlessness. This treatment was indeed desirable in *Feierabend*, 'Ach wie ist mein Arm so schwach' (Ex. 3. 'Die Schöne Müllerin') but in this song a sense of exhaustion is conveyed by more subtle means. The semi-quavers should be heavy—I mean heavy in the sense they should be dull and lacking in animation. The intervals from 'wie' to 'müd', from 'da' to 'ich', from 'zur' to 'Ruh' are laboured, while the octave drop on 'lege' is the personification of weariness. Laboured again is the step by step climb from 12 to 15. 'Wege' may be the apex but the *diminuendo* in the preceding bar returns us to the song's normal dynamic —*piano*. These ingredients are well considered and then the whole is sung *legato* with breaths only as I have marked.

Toilsome strides are a feature of *Rast* they are anticipated in the pianoforte treble of the introduction and are repeated ceaselessly throughout the song as in 15, 16.

Ex.3

Under the singer's 'Die Füsse frugen nicht nach Rast' (my feet needed no rest) 17, 18, the pianoforte's twinges of pain seem to belie the words, for later when he sings 'der Rükken fühlte keine Last' (my back felt no burden) it is so forlorn (and marked *leise* and *pianissimo* for good measure) that we feel the poor man in his desire to get on, is indeed deluding himself.

Ex.4

der Rük-ken fühl-te kei-ne Last, der Sturm half fort mich we -hen,

But on no account must the performers be deluded. Although *sotto voce*, it is not to be sung with complacency but with an appreciation of those wide stretches on 'Rükken' and 'fühlte' and the drooping descent at 'keine Last'. The possessor of a charming *pianissimo* and smooth delivery may feel that this is not a particularly difficult passage to accomplish, but it is important he should make us feel that great effort is needed. If he is really living in the song he will not throw the phrase away, a temptation that does not arise at 24 where it is marked *stark*; here he really needs to exert himself. He remembers too that the passage is to be reiterated with greater emphasis at bar 30 for which he would be wise to hold an ounce of *forte* in reserve.

The pianoforte swells mightily to support the voice in the *crescendi* on 23 and 29.

The two quatrains we have looked at, take up a page of Schubert's score, and the last two are a repetition so far as the music is concerned.

'I found shelter in a charcoal burner's cabin but my limbs still ache and my wounds smart. My heart, so bold in strife and storm, in this quiet moment stirs and burns within me.'

Expression marks are not quite identical, the second section (37) starts *pianissimo* and the *crescendo* 'so brennen ihre wunden' (44, 45) is sharper. Bar 44, corresponding with 14 in Ex. 2 now has a biting C flat in place of the earlier natural.

The postlude, still with its *staccato* quavers and its stressed second beats sinks in volume and gradually slows down with a pause before— and on—the final chord.

Appoggiaturi in bars 20 and 50 are treated as they were in bars 10 and 38 in *Irrlicht*.

XI. FRÜHLINGSTRAUM

WE LEFT our poor friend with a sheltering roof over his head and a hope that he would find some repose for his aching limbs. Nothing could succeed *Rast* more aptly than *Frühlingstraum* where he tells us he has sweet dreams and, awakening in the early morning sees frost patterns like flowers on the window pane. In Müller's original *Winterreise* this song was the twenty-first in the cycle. Fortunately the order of this and other poems was changed, whether by Schubert or not is uncertain, but the present order is greatly to the benefit of the cycle as a whole and in this particular case is logical.

Winterreise in the opinion of the writer is the greatest song cycle ever written. In it Schubert overcame problems—though he did not recognize them as problems—which would have been insurmountable to any other of the recognized masters of the Lied. Nevertheless, and love it as we may, the fact remains that it is a melancholy story for all its infinite variety and for this reason, if for no other, it is vital that the singer seizes every opportunity to give us lyrical and relaxed singing. Such occasions occurred in *Der Lindenbaum*, will come in *Täuschung*, they even appear momentarily in the nocturnal tramping *Im Dorfe*, and are here in this song.

Frühlingstraum is *a b c a b c* in form: the *a* sections are blissfully dream-like in character, the middles are rude awakenings to reality, while sad resignation is the tenor of the final *c*'s. Each section has its own tempo independent of its neighbour.

The opening fourteen bars are so innocent and charming they might have been plucked from one of the sprightly 'Maid of the Mill' songs.

'I dreamt of gay blossoms blooming in May time, of green meadows and of birds' song.'

Ex.1

(♩.= 48 or 52)

There is a disarming simplicity about it. Of course this introduction could be read quite easily at sight though justice cannot be done to Schubert by such a superior approach. The little tune flows along sweetly and unpretentiously with a graceful inflexion at 2 and with unfussy feathery grace notes in 3: the left hand's *staccato* on the third and sixth quavers should not be neglected. It is all *pp* yet within that compass, bars 1 and 2 climb, bars 3 and 4 descend; a gentle rise and fall. Pedal of course is used. Having thought along these lines and practised it assiduously, the pianist may find that the playing is likely to become too studied, too wooden. What can he do? He leaves it alone, for it deserves to sound as fresh as the dew in springtime. When he returns to it he will find that his thought and time have not been wasted—we shall hear when this music is performed that he loves it; the singer too will be inspired.

We must be made to forget the anguish of heart and bodily pain of the love-lorn man. The singer's tone is silvery and smooth. Only for fourteen bars will it last, so let him be sentimental if he will—there is hardly time enough for this slight extravagance to be perceived let alone criticized. 'Bunten Blumen' must be enjoyed and treated as the pianist treated bar 2. 'So wie sie wohl blühen im Mai' becomes entrancing if the first and fourth beats are made a little longer and the semiquavers very light; again a leisurely course from 'im' to 'Mai' is taken as if reluctant to leave 'im'.

The suspended E in the above is stretched, helping the rapid glancing semiquavers of 'von' to swoop down buoyantly and smoothly as a bird.

Sweet dreams end in a long silence, a silence shattered by the harsh crowing of cocks,—'my eyes opened, it was cold and dark, and the crows croaked on the roof'.

So sudden is the transition from fantasy to reality, tranquillity to commotion that we are startled. The singer's attack is made sharper by a quicker tempo ($\quarternote. = 76$) and by giving an edge to the thin vowels of 'Hähne' and 'Kräten', 'schrieen' and 'Raben'. No attempt is made to make the tone mellifluous; each short phrase—cut off abruptly without finesse—mounts to the raven's croaking in 21. The pianoforte contributes to this racket by its screeching in 16 and 18, 22 and 24,

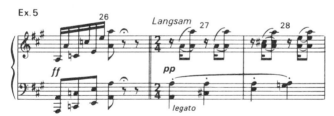

Ex. 5

and these discords are blatant. Bar 26 loses its effect entirely if the broken octaves are picked out with care, they must be played with *brio*.

Bars 27, 28 belong to section *c* and I include them in the above example for two reasons:

First to draw attention again to the silence after the clattering octaves. These silences occur four times in the song and Schubert has given them *fermati* very distinctly, they are there for dramatic effect. In a

large and over-resonant hall the *fortissimo* overtones in 26 and 70 will
take longer to disappear and the pianist must be content to wait until
they have died away before proceeding.

Secondly, they suggest how closely the accompaniment all through
these ensuing seventeen bars resembles, though at a slower tempo, that
of *Rast*—as if weariness once again had overcome the dreamer.

In the growing light the man sees frost figures on the window, shapes
that remind him of leaves and flowers. He asks himself 'Who painted
them? Why laugh that a dreamer imagines flowers in the winter?'

Half awake he longs to be wholly asleep again, to dream and to
forget the present. This section is all *pp*, but it must be wan, with a
rueful expression in 41 as voice and pianoforte *crescendo* together, with
some bitterness on 'Winter'.

The octaves and the accompanying treble in 42, 43 die away, each
less in weight than the other. Since the level is already *pp*, the pianist
gives a little more tone on the first octave to make his *diminuendo*
possible.

'Etwas bewegt' at 44 indicates a return to *tempo primo*, it is the bar
linking section *c* to the return of *a*, and trips airily back to the subject.
Whether it should be *tempo subito* or *poco a poco accelerando* into tempo
at 45 is a matter for the artists to discuss. It has been my habit for years
to strike tempo immediately, but latterly I have been more inclined to
the gradual quickening. Either procedure is acceptable provided the
difference in colour between the sombre 42, 43 bars and the sprightly
44 (*staccato* with pedal) is heard.

'I dreampt of love requited, of embracing and kissing my darling. But now, startled into wakefulness by the cock's crowing, I sit here alone with eyes closed and recall that dream.'

Since *Frühlingstraum* is strophic there is little more to be said. And yet I must add that the close of the last quatrain plumbs the very depths of despair: 'When will those leaves on the window turn green? When shall I hold my love in my arms again?'

I do not think there is a situation in all the cycle where the poor fellow is more crushed than this. There must be no semblance of a *crescendo* on the rising phrase 'Wann halt ich mein Liebchen im Arm'? (83) it is unmitigated *pp*. Never would I suggest, that the singer should become inaudible but here he is as near to it as may be. If he has lived in and believed in what he has been singing, if he has sung with heart as well as mind, if he has sung without mannerism or arrogance, in other words if he is a true artist his hearers will be sharpened to acute concentration and will not miss one note, one word.

XII. EINSAMKEIT

'As A dark cloud is wafted by a gentle breeze so do I drift aimlessly with sluggish steps, dumb and alone, in the sunshine. No one greets me. O calm air, O sunshine! When the tempests howled and raged I was not so unhappy as this.'

Sunshine and clear skies seem to the wanderer to be a mockery. Nature in its roughest mood is more welcome: his spirit responds eagerly to the savagery of *Der stürmische Morgen* (Stormy morning) and the buffeting in *Mut* (Courage).

Ex.1

A picture of the trudging footsteps is seen in the introduction. Note the slur over the bass chords, a *staccato* touch is used for these but with the sustaining pedal; only the treble in 3, 4, 5 is played *legato* and should stand out in contrast above the dull plodding bass with the *fp* (5) much more pronounced than the time stresses. After this the accompaniment —until bar 22—keeps in the background, only the heavy treads in 15, 16 and 19, 20 should be felt.

In *Frühlingstraum* the singer's final strains were forlorn and faint but now, with idle thoughts and fancies shaken off, the man is on the move. The singer communicates this at once by the firmness of his line and by its weight. The instruction is *pp* which suffices for the pianoforte but is not enough for the voice.

Ex. 2

Wie ei - ne trü-be— Wol - ke durch hei-tre Lüf-te— geht, wenn

in der Tan-ne— Wip - fel ein mat-tes Lüft-chen weht:

Intonation must be watched at 8 and 12. So often the C sharp fails to reach dead centre by being attacked from below. The note must be pitched high and attacked from above (the fact that the preceding note lies lower in the stave has nothing to do with the argument).

There is a natural tendency to increase tone with the rise, and decrease with the fall of the phrases, a practice which the patient reader is aware I often endorse, but here no conscious effort should be made to do this; the tone is spread evenly in weight along these passages. I hope my reason will be made clear later.

Fairly strict tempo is held until we come to 17 and 21

Ex. 3

so zieh ich mei-ne— Stra-ße da - hin mit trä-gem Fuß, durch

hel-les, fro-hes Le - ben ein - sam und oh - ne Gruß.

'Mit trägem Fuss' (dragging step)—'ohne Gruss' (ungreeted) are the kernels of these two stretches. They are emphasized—not by a loudening of the tone—but by holding back the movement which till now has been regular. (Hugo Wolf would have described it 'etwas zurück-haltend'). This slight dragging of the tempo loses its effect if pre-tentious swelling of tone is made on to 'Strasse' (16) and 'Leben' (20). This is the reason for my aversion—in this instance—to these customary inflections; also they tend to detract from the great *crescendi* that are in the offing. Each phrase should be sung in one breath if possible. It may be some consolation to the singer to remind him that we have two beats to the bar—not four; ♩ = 42 approximately.

Up to this point the wanderer has plodded on with phlegmatic resignation but now a transformation comes as he is seized by an upsurge of spirit and raises his voice vehemently at his miserable plight.

The link between these contrasts in temper lies in the pianoforte's very short but vital interlude. For a moment the pianist takes the reins. At 22, 23 each note, albeit bound one to the other in absolute *legato*, must have a vibration of its own, demands a concentrated energy of its own and then merges and combines with its neighbour to make the whole passage arresting in its intensity. As he climbs upwards to the singer's 'Ach' the player becomes more and more deliberate as if the hapless man were slowly stretching up his arms to invoke the heavens.

This preparation makes it possible for the singer to have freedom over the next two phrases which are sung *quasi recitative*. Much time is taken on 'Ach' and on 'so', time taken not only for the sake of expressive-ness but to conserve power, for lying in wait is the massive 'Als noch die Stürme tobten' which needs huge tone to soar above the thunder of the pianoforte.

Ex.5

The singer must see to it that 29, 30—and their repetition 41, 42—far outweigh in strength of tone the recitative bars.

It will be seen that 30 (similarly 42) has a quaver rest. Once again I beg the pianist to prolong rather than curtail this rest; the ring of the voice, the crash of the pianoforte must be well cleared—silence felt—before a move is made towards the most affecting moments of the song 'War ich so elend nicht' (I was less miserable than this) which is sung four times. And the performers sing this with all their hearts. No flimsy *piano* is wanted here, the voice is uplifted (so very different from the crushed condition of 'Wann halt ich mein Liebchen im Arm?' of *Frühlingstraum*); above all the final 'so elend nicht'

Ex.6

is a cry of anguish directed at the smiling pitiless sky. It is the singer's climax and he ignores the pianoforte's *diminuendo*. 'Nicht' is held no longer than is written to enable the *pianissimo* chords of the postlude to be heard but it should be enunciated with stinging explicitness.

Baritones will be pleased to know that Schubert, having first written *Einsamkeit* in D minor, later preferred it in B minor.

XIII. DIE POST

IN THESE essays I have referred frequently and with good reason to Richard Capell's *Schubert's Songs* (Duckworth Ltd), nevertheless and with respect I cannot find myself in total agreement with the author at all points—nor, I am sure, would he expect it. *Einsamkeit* which I consider to have eloquence and grandeur is a secondary song in Capell's estimation. *Die Post* he writes 'does well enough in Müller's sequence. Schubert's setting would be perfect as a detached song, but as it stands, its lightness is out of keeping with the tragic wanderer who is soon to say "Ich bin zu Ende mit allen Träumen".' Schubert had completed the first twelve songs of *Winterreise* in February 1827 and did not tackle the remaining dozen (starting with *Die Post*) till six months later: I add this in fairness to Capell to justify his contention that the composer 'did not call to mind at once the passion and significance with which he had been charging the (previous) songs', and that the call of the horn is too cheerful.

This is a strophic song *a b a b* in form, and undoubtedly the first and third verses are lively. But liveliness is not synonymous with cheerfulness.

It was an old custom for the guard on a stage coach to sound the horn on approaching a town and the call he blew was, I imagine, always the same or pretty much the same, nor was it calculated to bring happy smiles to the faces of its hearers. One can say that our friend was crazy to allow his heart to leap at the sound of the post horn and then sink at the thought there was no letter for him. How could there be any

expectation when no one knew where he had roved? Of course he is
crazy—but he still watches and wonders.

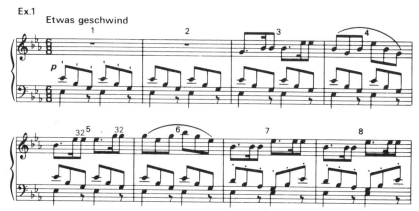

In this introduction, bars 3, 5, 7, 8 need a brassy quality in the treble.
How can this be done when the prevailing tonal level is *piano*? The
answer is *una corda*: it needs a *forte* touch with stiff fingers but with the
essential aid of the soft pedal. Bars 4 and 6 are slurred and only here is
the sustaining pedal used. I regard these two bars as parenthetical with
the horn blower silent; he is not a virtuoso and is heard only (with that
brazen sound) in 3, 5, 7, 8.

The lonely man is caught unawares by these noises, his heart beats
quicken.

It is tempting for the singer to respond with eager flashing eye to the infectious rhythm of clattering hooves and horn calls but he must abide by the *p* sign in bar 9. His rhythmic energy must indeed be precise, but it is not a cheerful energy, it is wide-eyed, startled. By restraining his tone at his entry he is able without undue effort to excite us by his *crescendo* up to the top note on 'Herz' (now in the key of D flat).

Once again as in the 6/8 of *Frühlingstraum* it is the short quavers that are lighter in weight. The thought behind it is of two beats to the bar rather than six; this will give point, for instance, to 'Strasse'—'Post-horn'—'hoch'—'Herz'.

Ex. 3

What a short lived animation it proves to be. After the *diminuendo* on 'Herz' (and to the repeated words of 13, 14, 15) the bass in the pianoforte as shown above takes us down step by step forecasting a much more chastened mood.

In fact the waiting man knows he is cherishing foolish hopes, knows the post brings no letter. 'Why do you throb so strangely, my heart?'

After one bar of silence section *b* starts in the minor, very softly and in complete contrast to the first verse.

Ex. 4

One is apt to adopt a slower tempo here. It is unnecessary: the absence of those energetic dotted quavers gives the impression, in any case, that the pace has slowed down.

The vocal line is *legato* now, even the rests in 28 do not seem to interrupt the flow; they should be 'thought through' with no breath taken, the tone dark. The smart on 'drängst' (the chromatic passing note—with the pianoforte's help) should be keen. 'Wunderlich' (32) is not hurried but bar 33 is pushed along by the pianist, so that 'mein Herz' can be dwelt on slightly. There is an increase as marked on 34, but 35 fades away suggesting the futility of it all, a futility eloquently echoed in the accompaniment.

The words of this verse are repeated with much more spirit, almost impatiently as if the man were chiding himself. It rises to a pitch of excitement unequalled previously, culminating in

A high note as ringing as he pleases is wanted from the singer here but he does not allow it to impede the momentum.

The last verses—for all their animation—carry the plaintive reflection 'Yes, the post comes from my beloved's town. My heart do you long to know how she fares'?

'Wo ich ein liebes Liebchen hat' is sung as though the man were unaware of its implication (this is subject *a* again, Ex. 2) but when repeated *pianissimo*

its purport goes straight to his heart and is sung with an aching regret. The song concludes in that vein. The question the man asks himself needs no answer. This is the point of *Die Post*.

Schubert, as Capell suggests, felt the necessity for a song of animation between *Einsamkeit* and *Der greise Kopf* but it is most certainly not at any moment a cheerful affair. The expression of hopeless longing—always in some form or another in all the cycle—is here with its smart. This is the message, and the singer must communicate it and in doing so rebut the suggestion that the song is out of keeping with the rest.

I take ♩. = 80 to 88 to be the basic speed.

XIV. DER GREISE KOPF

'THE FROST has covered my hair during the night and it pleased me that I had become a grey haired man. But when it thawed I saw my hair was still black and I shudder that I am still young and the grave so far away. Between dusk and dawn many a man's head has turned white. Who can believe that mine has not changed on this whole journey!'

Ex.1

The long rising and falling sweeps are one of the characteristics of this unusual song. What do they signify? Schubert supplies us with the answer in the last verse; it is found in the key phrase 'Von Abendrot zum Morgenlicht ward mancher Kopf zum Greise' (Between dusk and dawn many a man's head has turned white) for there we can appreciate that the intent of these long aching stretches is symptomatic of the constant anguish, interminable nights our poor friend endures.

Fortunately the performers know what it is all about before they start.

A big *crescendo* up to bar 3 is excessive in spite of the steep rise. The introduction should be played dynamically as marked, with A flat the apex made more important by a time-stress on the preceding semiquaver. Indeed a feeling of crispness in all semiquavers must be avoided, they are played with seriousness and if skimped will put the singer at a disadvantage. At rehearsal the pianist listens carefully to the singer's handling of this phrase and emulates it. Every *gruppetto* (or turn) whether in the vocal line or pianoforte is an *appoggiatura* with the first note of the turn coming on the beat and should be executed with deliberation even if occupying more time than is prescribed.

Ex.2

Now we see when compared with Ex. 1, how those upbeat semiquavers are here made twice as long. (I am not suggesting that the upbeats of the introduction be promoted from quarter-beats to half-beats, I am only drawing attention to their virtue.)

The singer exercises much more freedom than the pianist, his opening phrase is *a piacere*, sung in free time; recognizably three beats to the bar, yes, but they are not rigid beats. His breath after 'Schein' is taken with leisure and on the downward passage he makes his *appoggiaturi* on 'Haar gestreuet' with solemnity. Imposing though the arch is, a big *crescendo* would be an exaggeration for a slight swelling will happen inevitably without reinforcement from the singer.

'Hab mich sehr gefreuet' (pleased me) is different:

Ex.3

Here the words and the pianoforte counter melody (the tenor voice of the accompaniment) demand more enthusiasm from the singer. Obviously 'sehr gefreuet' needs more emphasis than 'und hab', the *crescendo* therefore does not start until after these high notes. Regrettably 'und hab' sometimes is dwelt on giving it unwarrantable lustiness at the expense of 'sehr gefreuet' which, finding the singer at the end of his breath, droops away disappointingly.

Disillusion comes with 'Doch bald ist er hinweggetaut' (soon when it thawed) and is delivered with impatience which, goaded by the *forte* chord in 19 develops into bitterness in 21, 22 (I shudder that I am still young).

Ex.4

Doch bald ist er hin-weg-ge taut, hab wie-der schwar-ze Haa-re, daß mir's vor mei-ner Ju-gend graut

Ever since 19 the volume has been growing, and 21 makes a *crescendo* with a seemingly uncontrolled quickening of the pace on to 'graut'. I use 'seemingly' advisedly for it is only the bitter wanderer whose impatience runs away with him, the singer always has the rhythm under control and, consistent with the quickening and loudening, hammers out relentlessly those dotted quavers and semiquavers.

'Graut' is the tonal climax of the song. Arrived there, the pianist pulls back the movement to give his partner a longer tenancy on the big note and in order to prepare for the coming of a more lugubrious thought.

The wretched sentiment that the grave is too far off is underlined by the clash of the G in the voice with the F sharp in the bass (26), a discord not to be resolved too facilely; it needs half a beat to itself, its discomfort must be driven home to the hearer.

I recommend, in the example above, that the *appoggiaturi* (in the accompaniment only) be converted to *acciaccaturi*, the small notes to be run off before the beat. This is a personal preference. Whichever way the artists decide to play these the pianist should bear in mind that they are reminders of the shuddering climax on 'graut'.

As will be seen in Ex. 2 the fourth verse begins by a repetition of the theme. But here the music must sound more significant than when the song started; these words (from dusk to dawn etc.) are the raison d'être of Schubert's arching passages and are sung with this in mind. (The text of the sermon!)

Once again we have voice and pianoforte in contrary motion in 38, 39 but this time more expansively.

Ex. 6

auf die - ser gan-zen Rei-se, auf die - ser gan-zen Rei - - se!

The repetition of the words in 40, 41 is a positive *forte*: 'ganzen' (entire) must tell us at once what an unending journey it has seemed to the sufferer.

For a postlude we have bars 3, 4 played again, but now with much more freedom and with the utmost expressiveness on that very slow *appoggiatura*.

XV. DIE KRÄHE

EXCEPT FOR the prelude and postlude, the treble in the accompaniment throughout this sinister song is like the flapping wings of the bird—a flapping that should always be evident—while the left hand keeps time with the voice constantly, sometimes doubling the vocal line.

In the voice part, one note attaches itself to the next with almost relentless insistence (*molto legato* describes it precisely, but I too wish to make clear *my* meaning with relentless insistence). In *Einsamkeit* I submitted that the tone be spread evenly over each note in the phrase, disregarding the line's rise and fall, and this applies here. We do not look for the high point, the singing should be without nuance; the revelation of the man's grim musing is enough of itself.

'A crow has been following me since I left the town, flying above my head. Crow, strange creature that you are, will you not leave me alone? Are you minded to prey upon my prostrate body? Well, it is not much farther to my journey's end so perhaps you will be the one true friend till death.'

Ex.1

Attention is arrested immediately by the dissimilarity of tessitura in the pianoforte between this and the previous song. The high treble should have a shrill quality and be very clear cut. Tempo remains unvaried in the introduction (I suggest ♩ = 44) with no hint of a *rallentando* before the entry of the voice.

In contrast to the accompaniment's two bar phrases, the singer's are of four bars (6 to 9 and 10 to 13). To span these in a single breath is meaningful, almost menacing, for it conveys in conjunction with the resolute *legato* the persistence of the tireless bird—always watching, always looming overhead. No weakening in volume, therefore, should be allowed on 'gezogen' (9) and 'geflogen' (13).

When the harassed man cries out at his pursuer, the nature of the singing alters.

These ejaculations put at first in a suppliant manner (16 to 19) are pitiful and are low in volume. This is the quietest stretch in the song. Only the slightest *crescendo—diminuendo* is made at the pleading 'Willst mich nicht verlassen?' On the other hand the *crescendo* at 20 gets more excited and much more querulous so that when we come to the dreadful suggestion 'meinen Leib zu fassen?' the poor man is crazed. To have resisted quickening the tempo during these wrought-up bars would have been less than human; acceleration seems to happen naturally and is acceptable provided it is not overdone for, quite suddenly, the pianist finds he has one bar only in which to ease the pace back to the first tempo.

At this bar he not only recovers *tempo primo* but the quieter mood as well. This ushers in the singer's four bar phrase 'Well, it is not much farther' etc. and again the vocal line is *molto legato*.

We come now to the climax, a huge *crescendo* on to 'Grabe' with the pianoforte treble high and shrill.

'Grabe' is delivered with ringing sonority, the word must be clearly and, yes, uncomfortably appreciated by the hearer. Let the singer consider too his passage on to the second syllable. Would a clean step down (from 32 to 33) be a true reflection of inner tumult? No, it needs a *portamento*. The slide from G to E would be obnoxious if it were allowed too much time; it is made at the last possible moment and so quickly that the ear is hardly aware it has taken place. 'Treue' in 36 also has a *portamento*, to step down neatly from the first to the second syllable without it would be too bad to be true.

The postlude is a repetition of the introduction but an octave lower. It needs no *rallentando* though a hold up with pedal before the final chord is suggested. **Ex. 5**

The bass notes, sinking down, are to be noticed and so is the B natural in 42. Faint echoes of the wanderer's grim idea 'meinem Leib zu fassen' are suggested by that repeated middle C. It is a sinister pecking.

The accompaniment to *Die Krähe* differs in one respect from all other songs in *Die Winterreise.*

When one considers *Wohin, Liebesbotschaft, Auf dem Wasser zu singen, Der Jüngling an der Quelle,* it is impossible to imagine more felicitous settings. We should be outraged if any attempt were made by any other composer to set them differently. Had Richard Strauss thought to put these verses to music his *arpeggios* would have cascaded all over the pianoforte in the most opulent manner, the temptation would have been irresistible to him. Surprisingly in one whose knowledge of and intimacy with the instrument and its possibilities were unrivalled, Schubert's infectious joy in ripple and flow is accomplished with very little fuss and within a confined compass on the keyboard. While the bass in his accompaniments is unrestricted, the treble is kept within narrow bounds in nearly all his songs.

What was the reason for this? Was the tone of the pianoforte in Schubert's time unsatisfactory to him in *altissimo* when coalesced with the voice? Did it lack the singing quality he wanted? Was it a disagreeable sound?

If the answer to these questions is in the affirmative it explains why he would be disposed to resort to the high register for the pathetic mood of *Die Krähe* finding it a simulation of the shrill cries of the bird, but would avoid it in joyous songs of young love, of running streams and smiling flowers.

At all events the treble here in this wonderful song lies most of the time *in alt* (that is, the octave above the stave) and is allowed occasionally to wing over *in altissimo.*

XVI. LETZTE HOFFNUNG

THE MERE appearance of the introduction suggests a fluttering falling movement. It is weightless and it is wayward. One can be certain that Schubert at his instrument did not perform it with metronomic precision—here it was hurried, there held back—as capriciously as a leaf in the wind.

It is instructive to examine the authentic marks; time stresses are shewn in the first half of the prelude but not after. I think the composer was indicating as clearly as it is possible the way he wished the *rubato* to be shaped; bars 1, 2 taking more time than 3, 4 though the *fermata* in 4 is made quite long. The tone never rises above *pp* and the sustaining pedal is eschewed. It is dry and withered as a dead leaf.

'Here and there on the trees a late leaf is still to be seen. Often I look at those trees and fix my gaze on one leaf. On this leaf I pin my hopes, and when the wind plays with it I tremble lest it fall. If it drops, my hope goes with it and I too fall to the ground and weep, weep on the grave of my hope.'

Ex. 2

To some extent the vocal line is like the introduction with the singer's 'Hie und da ist an den Bäumen' avoiding regularity of tempo; it must be clearly articulated. Perhaps the violinist's *spiccato* could be brought to mind (the bow bouncing on the string) when treating the quavers; the latter must be fitful and to join them smoothly to each other would be undesirable—on the other hand *staccato* would be too flippant. As opposed to this 'Manches bunte Blatt zu sehn' is very *legato* and this is indicated by the slur marked in the pianoforte. The second phrase is handled in the same way, time being allowed on the important 'Gedanken'. These passages are each contained in one breath.

Up to this moment the singer has been expressing the scene. What follows now—despite the pianoforte maintaining its wintry *staccato*—is dealt with differently. 'I fix my gaze on one leaf, I hang my hopes on it' etc. calls for more and more intensity with each advance. The watcher is deadly serious and in consequence the detached style of the opening will not do—these are short phrases admittedly but are sung more smoothly especially the triplet on 'hänge' bar 16.

This difference in style is arresting enough of itself without increase of tone; the *crescendo* begins at 19, but the singer waits for the dramatic 'Ach und fällt das Blatt zu Boden' to make this his salient point. His sights have been fixed on it since 15. It is approached by the accompaniment's semiquavers of 23 (with pedal)—the leaf quivering in the wind—and by the *crescendo* (now without pedal) at 25.

The *diminuendo* on 'Blatt zu Boden' is not to be made expressly—with that octave drop of the voice it will happen anyhow.

I have included bar 24 in Ex. 4 because of the rests, four quavers in length and not to be overlooked.

Preparation should be made for the *Etwas langsamer* of 29, 30 where the singer strikes a new and solemn tempo, and the pianist shows consideration for his partner by not rushing headlong to the brink but by easing the pace into it at 28. *Un poco ritard* is marked in the score at 29 but I feel it necessary for it to be effected a bar earlier.

At 'fällt mit ihm' etc. the player listens attentively to the singer's shaping of this phrase since he tries to match it immediately afterwards. The significance of these two bars, so low in tone, so crushed in spirit, is that they are in juxtaposition to the biggest *forte* of the song 'fall ich selber mit zu Boden'. It is imperative for the pianist to make *tempo subito* at 31.

This is so desperate that the singer has no choice but to give the top G flat all the tone he possibly can in the short spell he stays on it.

Although a highly dramatic pitch has been reached here, the emotional

consummation is still to come, and is a climax, expressed in the simplest terms, piercing the heart. It is a blaze of genius.

As before (28) the pianist in 34 preceding these immortal moments, makes his contribution with his *diminuendo* and a slight lingering on his dominant chord, on which third beat he uses his sustaining pedal. These measures pave the way for the singer, more than that they serve to warn the listener that if he has tears he should prepare to shed them now.

'Wein auf meiner Hoffnung Grab' is the only line in all the verses that is repeated, it meant much to Schubert and it means much to the singer who pours all his soul into it. But he will not shed tears, his tears were shed in rehearsal. If he hopes to move his hearers he must exercise control over his feelings otherwise he will have no control over his voice. His responsibility keeps his emotions in check.

These phrases are *molto legato* and need the most melting tone. Much feeling can be put into bars 35 to 38 by maintaining the *piano* as marked and by avoiding unnecessary nuances. Breath can be taken imperceptibly at 36 to help the unhurried triplet on 'Hoffnung' and to allow latitude on the consonants of 'Grab', a word enunciated with utmost distinctness. At 39 there is of course a heart-swelling *crescendo* (not approaching the violence of 32) and with a *portamento* from the high G (without shortening it) on to the E flat.

The accompanying chords of 41, 42—before resuming the falling-leaf motif—are detached under the sustained vocal line. But the last despairing plaint, the *fp* at 45 in the postlude, is not to be confused with these lifeless chords or with the falling leaves in 43, 44.

Ex. 7

Here the pianist brings a warm humanity into play. The *fp*, melting *diminuendo* and sustaining pedal combine to make this an affecting moment, a faint memory of the singer's heart-rending 'Wein, wein'.

XVII. IM DORFE

WHEN THE composer sang and played the whole cycle to his friends for the first time, the songs with one exception were beyond their understanding; that exception, we are told, being *Der Lindenbaum. Letzte Hoffnung* and *Im Dorfe* must have nonplussed them. Many masterpieces from Schubert were written before these two songs but for inventive imagination they bear comparison with the very greatest.

It is night time and the wanderer passes through a village. The dogs roused by his footsteps welcome him with barking and the rattling of their chains. 'The people are fast asleep' he reflects, 'dreaming of things that are out of their reach, finding refreshment in visions good and bad, until morning puts an end to their sleeping'.

Ex.1

A picture is brought to mind by this extraordinary introduction. In the bass is heard the growling of dogs and the sound of them straining at their chains. It can also be a simulation—when the singer refers to sleepers in their beds—of snoring, especially with that abrupt *appoggiatura* as if a man were awakened with a sudden start. This figure predominates, with the repetitive treble chords heard, or rather felt, only in the background. Yet a muffled quality of sound is wanted; it is, after all, in the middle of the night and instinctively one moves about without wishing to disturb, therefore *una corda* is necessary except in the *crescendo* at 3 and at 6 where a slight swelling of tone foreshadows the voice's 'Es bellen die Hunde'. The sustaining pedal is held in the first half of each bar but is released immediately after the *appoggiatura* to give effect to that impressive silence of five quavers duration.

Ex.2

For his words to make sense it would be absurd to sing 'The dogs are barking' in a clandestine manner; the singer listens to the *crescendo* in the first half of bar 6 on the pianoforte and judges how much tone he needs to give. 'Bellen', 'Hunde' are made prominent and explain to a great extent the mysterious rumblings of the introduction: they are euphonious and are grateful to the voice even though their implication is disagreeable. But 'rasseln'! (rattling). Here is an ugly word and no attempt should be made to beautify it, there is a rasping suggestion about it. And then look at the gaping intervals in 8, 9 'es schlaffen die Menschen in ihren Betten', if ever there were a suggestion of yawning, here it is. Schubert did not write such a vocal line by accident.

At 11, 'Träumen sich manches' etc. is *pp* and kindlier in feeling following the somewhat bitter tones of the opening—the *p* in 11 caters for it. The leaning note or *appoggiatura* on 'haben' (13) is a full dotted crotchet as elsewhere in the song. 'Guten und Argen erlaben' has a *crescendo* but thereafter the music reverts to a *pp* for 'in the morning all has vanished'. This heralds a transformation, short but magical.

For a brief spell the wanderer is taken out of himself and ponders
without envy on the lot of these slumbering villagers.

'Ah well, in their dreams, at least, they tasted hope and will find it
again when they return to their pillows.'

The singer remembers the warmth he wanted in *Der Lindenbaum*, with the difference that in this instance the texture is much less solid; the line is tenuous and needs the most delicate inflexions. Rises and falls in 21 and 23 are minute and he listens for the refreshing soprano voice of the pianoforte in the second half of 21, 23, 24, 25. His singing of 'hoffen und hoffen'—stressing slightly the first syllable—paradoxically suggests what little cause there is for hope so far as he is concerned.

Bars 18 and 19, so deceptively easy in appearance are a test for the accompanist, his musicality can be assessed by his playing of them. The semiquavers are played without pedal, and from the first, in strict tempo each one becoming less in tone. This *diminuendo* is a tall order considering the bar begins *pp*; it demands careful listening and sensitivity of touch. At 19 (now with pedal) comes a ray of light, rising and falling; it is welcoming the singer's 'Je nun'.

This section is ended by a cadenza-like passage on the pianoforte. Tranquillity is followed by ill-humour.

Ex.4

'Drive me off you barking creatures, do not allow me peace in hours that were meant for slumber! No matter, I have done with dreams, why should I linger among these sleepers?'

We see by the pianoforte's growling that the first subject is resumed. If the singer's 'Bellt mich nur fort' is not maledictory (though this is my reading of it) it is certainly stronger stuff than irritability and needs more tone than anywhere else in the song. Yes, the *crescendo* is not marked until 32, but the pianist starts it on 30 and unequivocally; without this encouragement the singer is left high and dry.

The outburst is short, for 35 'Ich bin zu ende mit allen Träumen', is quiet again and resigned. It would be incorrect to link 'zu ende' together under any circumstances, but here their separation gives the necessary finality to 'ende'.

'Why should I linger' etc. has a block harmony accompaniment which suggests physical fatigue, though the *crescendo* (not as marked in some editions) grows up to 'säumen'.

Even the dogs are heard only intermittently, having tired themselves of growling: their noise gets fainter and fainter as the village is left behind. This is graphically drawn in the postlude and played *a tempo* and with deliberation.

I would like here to recapitulate.

As well as wronging the composer I should be doing the singer a great disservice were he to take my rasping 'rasseln' and my yawning 'schlafen' too literally. These ideas, as I have said elsewhere, are at the back of his mind, and for the singer to spotlight them or make histrionics out of them would be reprehensible.

I have to add this postcript (with apologies to the serious student of Lieder who would not countenance them) since in some quarters these exaggerations—even studied movements of head or body—are considered outward and visible signs that the singer is 'living in the song'; in reality they betray a woeful lack of understanding and taste.

XVIII. DER STÜRMISCHE MORGEN

IF *Einsamkeit* expressed the fugitive's heaviness of spirit induced by calm bright weather, this stormy morning invigorates him and accords with his spleen.

'How the storm has torn the sky apart with the clouds fluttering in rags, and red fire flashing among them. This is the morning for me! My heart is painted in those raging skies; nothing but winter suits me —cold and furious winter.'

'Ziemlich geschwind' is the marking and I take this to be ♩ = 92 approximately, but then comes the injunction 'doch kräftig' (yet forcible). The score is certainly designed to be sung and played with power but we must bear in mind that *ff* does not make an appearance till half way through the song. Let me put it this way; although the storm clouds are out of control, the performers are not. This precept applies to rhythmic control even more than to judgement of dynamics.

I have indicated the basic speed but that is not to say that the measure is four-square, undeviating and stolid. The muscle inherent in the music is made more potent if allowed some elasticity, an elasticity to be exercised with discrimination.

Ex.1

Thus the second and fourth beats in bar 1 are longer than the first or third, and this gives the quavers a chance to make their *staccato* more telling. Bar 2 is quite different, here the semiquavers (beats one and two) are hurried up to the *sf* giving the diminished seventh more time— this is the apex of the climb. In short, the semiquavers are gusty and pedalled, the quavers spiky—they cannot be too *staccato*—and un-pedalled; the chords are thunderclaps.

Ex. 2

It would be difficult to sing 'Sturm zerissen' with the same *brio* that was heard in the introduction's semiquavers (it is quite easy on the pianoforte) without the enunciation becoming incoherent; the listener must be told the reason for this sudden eruption therefore it would be wise for the sake of clarity, if the singer handles the semiquavers with some prudence (they can still be aggressive) and he recompenses by giving fierce emphasis on 5. My recommendation for bar 4 applies equally to the semiquavers in 6. Truly I am concerned about the *melismata* which are met half a dozen times in the course of the song— the intrusive and deplorable 'H' must be kept out.

'Umher in mattem Streit' (7) has false accents in the accompaniment which the singer with his uniform *f* ignores; he tries to maintain his strength of tone when the vocal line drops rather low in 8.

And now comes our first *ff* (9).

Ex. 3

This lies so gratefully that as much tone is poured out as can be.

The sustaining pedal has been used at 10, but the chords in the first half of 11 seem to have more cutting edge if they are not bound together.

It will be noticed that I have written a crushed note to come before the beat (*acciaccatura*) in this bar; in Mandyczewski the semiquavers in the pianoforte move with the voice (as an *appoggiatura*) making it sound too comfortable. General practice is to play it as in the example above.

The singer should temporize by a slight decrease in volume at 'Mein Herz sieht an den Himmel' in order to give added force to

Ex. 4

which must be terrific.

XIX. TÄUSCHUNG

THE VIENNESE spirit, brought to light so deliciously in many Schubert songs is illustrated in *Täuschung* (Delusion) whose bewitching lilt falls gratefully on ear and mind after the tempestuous 'Stormy Morning'. Richard Capell explaining this surprising song quotes the Fool in King Lear 'Then they for sudden joy did weep, and I for sorrow sung'.

Not for the first time is our friend deluded, once it was the Will o' the wisp (*Irrlicht*)—here it is another lure; then he trudged on defying the fates to do their worst, now he follows the dancing gleam with irresponsible light-heartedness.

'A friendly light dances before me leading me off my path but I gladly follow its erratic drift. Ah, a fellow as woe-begone as I will seize on any airy decoy; it will take me beyond this icy darkness to a cheerful warm house wherein a dear one awaits me. Illusion—that is all I seek or can hope for.'

The enticing lure dances in the pianoforte introduction,

Ex.1

where the reiterated octaves teasingly persist right through the song. Bar 4 affords relief from the repetitious E naturals and E sharps and begs for the lightest and most graceful touch. These octaves are parenthetical under the voice—except in the two bar interludes between each vocal phrase—for it is the bass with its *staccato* and its stresses that makes us feel the pulse; these quavers are always on the dance. As for the stress on the second beat (we think of the tempo as two beats to the bar) this is made more intriguing if it is ever so slightly delayed; it is played over a score of times and never ceases to beguile.

Ex.2

Very few opportunities are granted in this cycle to the singer to put a smile into his tone. We have had fleeting moments of heart-warming recollection when pain was side-tracked; we recognized, alas, they were but moments and that sadness was waiting to renew its hold: in *Täuschung*—save for a passing reference lasting for two bars in the minor key—the wayfarer's unhappy lot is forgotten. He ignores the fact that his sentiments echoed in the two succeeding bars (8, 9)—(16, 17)—(20, 21) etc. etc. are being mocked by the pianoforte. (In these tiny interludes the treble is made more prominent; more 'top' is given to the octaves to give an added brightness, they are twinkling points of mockery to be relished by the pianist.) 'Ein Licht tanzt freundlich vor mir her' is sung with seemingly uninhibited pleasure and trips along lightly. Words can be indistinct if the singer does not enjoy them: to make them clear—without departing from the prevailing *piano*, the movement of lips and mouth must be generous. 'Tanzt' 'freundlich' 'folg' 'Kreuz' 'Quer' need energetic projection. The jocund mood is often enlivened by an *acciaccatura* or an *appoggiatura*, the former—a crushed note before the beat—is seen in 7, 15, and 32. An *appoggiatura* (19, 39) coming on the beat is generally accepted as taking half the time of the note following it; here however it is more in keeping with the spirit of the song if treated thus:

V. 1. ver-lockt den Wan - ders-mann.

The turn in bar 11 (Ex. 2) should be thrown away with easy nonchalance—again with the grace notes coming before the beat.

An abrupt or emphasized change of colour is unnecessary when we come to 'Ah! a fellow as miserable as I' (22, 23)

Ach! wer wie ich so e - lend ist, gibt gern sich hin der bun-ten List,

for the music's shift to the minor is enough of itself; it would be an over-elaboration to darken the tone—making too much of something the man is doing his best to forget. My phrase mark over 25, 26, 27 though the rest is observed, is to suggest that no breath be taken after 'gern'; even a quick breath deprives the phrase of eagerness.

We should be led to 'ein helles warmes Haus' (32, 33) in the gentlest way by the singer who makes an unhurried chromatic climb 28, 29, holds us in suspense on 'Grauss' then recaptures at 31 the former lilting flow.

die hin - ter Eis und Nacht und Graus ihm weist ein
hel - les, war - mes Haus

XX. DER WEGWEISER

A PRESSURE outside himself, invisible but inexorable seems to drive the pilgrim along a track unknown to him, to a goal he cannot determine. The tragedy of our friend is embodied in this song. We feel this relentless sway in the cruel discipline of the tempo which, once established, should be undeviating.

I have said on an earlier page that there is often one phrase in a composition which will supply the key to its tempo; in a song it should be a pace that makes it possible for the singer to move in technical comfort and to let us hear clearly what he is saying. The pianist's comfort is not—and of necessity cannot be—taken into account. Where do we find the clue in *Der Wegweiser*? I would say in the vocal line of bars 17, 18 (Ex. 2) (Allusion was made to this passage in the Preface for another reason, here I am only concerned with its execution). The 32nd notes must be vivid for they are, metaphorically the flick of the whip driving the movement on; too quick a tempo will render these notes trivial and the words unintelligible. A metronome beat of 88 to the quaver is a good tempo, the song lasts about three and three quarter minutes at this speed.

'Why do I avoid the road that other travellers take, and look for hidden tracks up in the hills amid the snow covered rocks? What wrong have I done that I should shun other men? What is the mad urge that thrusts me on into the wilderness? Signposts in plenty point to the towns yet I ignore them and press ever onwards, restless yet seeking peace. One signpost only is constant—ever before my eyes; it points to the one path I must take knowing I shall never return.'

Der Wegweiser does not pose exceptional problems of ensemble and balance for the performers but it does demand absolute accord between them in regard to its pace, and it is embarrassing to all concerned if the introduction sets off at a rate that is at variance with the speed the singer had in mind; then indeed the machinery creaks as one partner adjusts himself to the other. Thus the measure of understanding between the two is made apparent as soon as the singer gives voice.

Ex.1

The semiquavers in 5 and 7 (followed in the pianoforte bass) are heavy with fatigue and although one is aware that 'Wege' and 'andern' are high points they are sung without nuance—not made prominent. As if the man were forced along against his will, the motion seems involuntary and a grudging motion at that. Only in the pianoforte is there a slight rise and fall at 9, 10—(as *legato* as possible) and the stumbles in 12 and 14 made evident.

Ex. 2

At 'verschneite Felsenhöhn' the singer cannot help being influenced by the darkened colour as the pianoforte declines to the bass D flat; this coupled with the dejected alto harmony is a passage to make the heart sink. Then come the significant bass in 16 and the voice's repeats of it in 17, 18; the impact of these figures, the one in F minor followed at once by the same in G minor is portentous in its effect.

'What wrong have I done?' etc. returns to the *pp* level and is in the major; pitiful to start with, it rises to *f* at 'What mad urge impels me?'

Ex. 3

Pain at 'törichtes Verlangen' is heightened by the sudden halting of movement in the pianoforte for the first time in the song, and the singer makes us aware of the distress implied by his *fp*.

It is true that 33 is marked *pp* but the pianist looking ahead makes allowance for 35 where the transition to minor should be even more subdued.

The hiatus at 40 at the end of the interlude before the singer's entry has meaning—where the full stop in the introduction (bar 5) has not—

Ex. 4

for these three quaver rests give the impression that the wanderer has stayed his step and pauses to look around before saying 'Weiser stehen auf dem Wegen'.

We hear again with the third verse the main subject but at 52, 53 it makes an unexpected and typically Schubertian change.

Ex. 5

A comparison with Ex. 2 (bars 16, 17, 18) shows what has happened; the five note motif—F minor and G minor—remains this time in the accompaniment while the vocal line soars to a degree of poignant desperation without parallel in the rest of the song. 'Und suche Ruh' is the dynamic high point and the singer is prudish who allows the top note on 'Und' to be sung 'discreetly' in order to give pride of place to 'suche'; this would be a refinement calculated to rob the emotional moment of all truth. The conflict between the music's urge and the metrical demands of speech must be ignored. Schubert could easily have repeated the formula of the first verse but he rose above it; the words meant much to him but the music more. The accentuation on 'Und' may be displeasing to the pedants but Schubert's song sails on untrammelled and the singer is swept along by the might of it, gives it full heart and voice.

'One signpost ever before me' etc. is quieter and ill at ease, and is connected to the vehemence of the previous verse by a single repeated note in the pianoforte, a device used to link the first and second verses. (In function it is similar to the slender thread heard in *Im Dorfe*.)

This relentless monotone is continued by the singer for four bars, with a *crescendo* it is lifted to B flat, a monotone again, still further to D flat resolving at last to D natural. It is as if the walker were advancing with wide staring eyes, unseeing; propelled by the foreboding chromatic ascent of the pianoforte's bass.

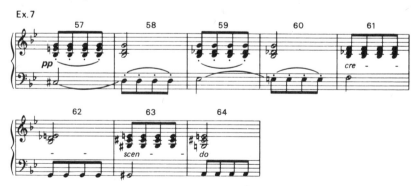

With those hypnotic monotones again in evidence the last verse is repeated, this time in less volume but made more ominous by the pincer movement closing in on the vocal line.

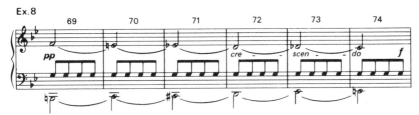

We have seen how the quaver movement has nearly always been present either in voice or pianoforte—prodding, prodding; but for the final 'die noch keiner ging zurück' though the tempo remains constant, the momentum is missing as if the straggler were unaware of motion.

      *   *   *

I beg the indulgent reader to allow me a postscript for I would like to raise a point concerning the pianoforte introduction.

It has always seemed unnecessary that the forward movement should be arrested by the tonic chord in bar 5, the stride is interrupted by a full stop before the singer can take up the tempo again. It is lèse-majesté to Schubert but a small voice within me says it would prefer bars 4 and 6 to proceed thus, cutting out bar 5 of the introduction:

It could be argued that there is a similar disjunction at bar 40 before the third verse but here the chord bringing the motion to a temporary halt is in the dominant and the car waits patiently for its resolution.

I objected, it may be recalled, to the *fermata* at the end of the introduction to *Das Wandern*, the first song in 'Die Schöne Müllerin' and suggested the singer should ignore it, should in fact show impatient eagerness to keep the tempo flowing. I feel the same applies to *Der Wegweiser*.

My position may be strengthened—and it is germane to the argument
—if I cite *Die Forelle* where again the rippling movement of the introduction is brought to an illogical stop. I have no hesitation in describing
this as illogical since in the Mandyczewski edition there is no introduction at all; the interlude between the first and second verse was
tacked on to the beginning as an afterthought—not, I believe by
Schubert—and it makes a wholly charming and most necessary preface
to the singer's tale. It is delicious but not when played as follows:

I submit bar 6 should be discarded, as in fact it is in the interlude and
that the singer's entry should be made on the last quaver of bar 5.
Happily my advice regarding *Das Wandern* and *Die Forelle* has been
adopted more often than not.

What of *Der Wegweiser*? Though unashamed, I have never pressed
my view on to the singer for one very good reason; the thought never
occurred to me until now when sitting down to write about this song.
It should be remembered that in performance the singer who adopted
the suggestion would risk being hauled over the coals by the critics,
none the less I should applaud the artist who shared my opinion and had
the courage to put it into execution.

XXI. DAS WIRTSHAUS

'I FOLLOWED a track that has brought me to a graveyard where, I told
myself, I would stay the night. Those green funeral wreaths might very

well be inviting signs of an inn where tired travellers could find refuge. Is it possible that the rooms are all reserved? I am tired to death; O cruel inn do you turn me out? Then on, on, I and my pilgrim staff.'

Das Wirtshaus with its conventionality, block harmony and tempered mood might well have been written by Mendelssohn and is the least remarkable composition in the cycle; indeed it almost becomes re-markable by reason of its stereotyped simplicity for in this respect it stands alone. Schubert judged the moment to perfection when the listener needed a sedative after the tearing experience of preceding songs, yet from the singer's point of view it is far from affording a temporary relaxation. Appearances are deceptive. The vocal phrases look short enough on the score but in practice, so slow is the tempo, they are protracted and call for strong support and firm breath control. Except for a short moment at the end when the voice rises to a *mf*, the dynamic range of the song is restricted from *pp* to *p*.

Not unlike an organ voluntary, thickness of texture characterizes Prelude and Postlude and the player simulates the *legato* touch of the organist over whom, however, he has one advantage, namely, he can give a little more weight or gentle pressure to the soprano voice, which should be heard above the lower voices (not to be over-emphasized, I did say 'a little more') it makes the sound less solid in quality.

As usual the time stresses are points of rest and bar 5 is played without a strict regard to tempo, the *gruppetto* is leisurely.

Ex. 2

A piacere being the nature of bar 5 the singer should be in no haste to make his *auftakt* after the dominant seventh chord.

The music of itself tells of a man who is sick unto death with weariness and it is unnecessary to gild the lily with darkened tone, rather the voice should be allowed to float quietly over the earnest accompaniment. Lightness of touch in general is needed on the semiquavers in the first two verses, those in 6 and 7 are instances, but there are exceptions for 'einkehren' (8) and 'Wandrer' (14) are made expressive by deliberation.

Apart from the commas in the text, breath can be taken after 'Totenkränze' (12)—'laden' (14)—'Hause' (18) and it is certain they will be needed if the tempo is of requisite slowness. Only the first phrase of all (6, 7) should be contained in one span.

The pianoforte's sigh in the soprano at 7 should not pass unheeded though the notes are parenthetical; of more significance are the alto E flat in 6 and D flat in 8 which are transferred to the soprano in verse 2 like a superimposed counterpoint sung by the trebles in a choir.

Ex. 3

If possible the third verse should be less in weight, weaker than before: in answer to the forlorn 'Sind denn in diesem Hause die Kammen all besetz?' the nadir of all hope and physical endurance is reached.

Ex. 4

bin matt zum Nie-der-sin -ken, bin töd-lich schwer ver-letzt.

Temptation to *crescendo* on to the high 'matt' should be resisted, much more meaning is conveyed if the note is *pp* and is allowed more time so that its import is not lost on the listener; 'tödlich schwer' too seems to ask for pressure, the pain of the discord appears to demand it but again the singer would be wise to disregard the impulse, to make a *crescendo* of the smallest degree suggests an energy which is in direct contradiction to the words. No, the voice should be colourless, drained of vitality; this does not imply that the voice is deprived of support, for when employing *mezza voce* the singer needs to exercise more control than ever.

He who follows my advice will find it demanding, for it is far easier to dilate on 'matt' and 'tödlich', but if he has looked ahead and plotted his course he will be aware that emotional urgency should be deferred until the final verse. It is an urgency strongly suggested by the interlude before 'Cruel Inn'.

Ex. 5

O un-barm-herz-ge Schen-ke,

These bars tell of a change in the wanderer's mood, a desperation now seizes him and grows in intensity reaching its summit in bar 27.

Ex. 6

Nun wei-ter denn, nur wei -ter, mein treu-er Wan-der-stab, nun

wei-ter denn, nur wei-ter, mein treu-er Wan-der-stab!

A philosophical acceptance of fate maybe, but there is no mistaking the agonized emergence of the last 'nun weiter', nor does it matter—since the word 'weiter' is being uttered for the fourth time (27)—if the semiquavers on 'nur' are expanded in order to allow a *portamento* from the F to the D. To make this *portamento* is human.

The last verse being charged with weighty dejection prompts the pianist to continue in the same strain at the beginning of his postlude; he quietens down by degrees to a *pp* ending.

To atone for what may be deemed my cool appraisal of *Das Wirtshaus* at the beginning of this essay let me say without equivocation that I find the song deeply moving.

XXII. MUTH

This is another case where Schubert's change in the order of the poems as set out by Wilhelm Müller shows to advantage for it was originally the penultimate song; it is possible that this was considered too frenzied a mood as a stepping-stone to the miraculous valediction of *Der Leiermann*.

'If the snow flies in my face, I dash it off. If my heart wails within me I sing gaily for I pay no heed to its lamentations. Only fools lament; so, blithely on into the world scorning wind and weather! If God has forsaken us on earth, we ourselves must be gods.'

Again, as in '*Der stürmische Morgen*', his conflict with the elements rouses our friend to exhilarated defiance.

Ziemlich geschwind would be approximately $\downarrow$ = 96 and the pianist plunges into his introduction with fury.

Ex.1
Ziemlich geschwind, kräftig

The *staccato* chords in 1 and 2 are rude bumps and their jarring effectively delays the forward march, but bars 3 and 4 repay the loss with exuberance and it is in these two bars that the basic tempo is established. Always the rhythm must be sinewy; elasticity is sought by the singer and player in every phrase, for the spirit goes out of the music if it becomes square. In the vocal line for instance.

Ex.2

Fliegt der Schnee ___ mir ins Ge - sicht,

Ex.2a

Wenn mein Herz ___ im Bu-sen spricht,

'If the snow flies in my face' (5–7) and 'If my heart wails' (12–14) are challenges and are held with a tight rein but these challenges are scornfully dismissed by the semiquavers in 8 and 15,

Ex.3

schüttl ich ihn ___ her - un - ter.

Ex.3a

sing ich hell und mun - ter;

semiquavers which, echoed by the pianoforte, are thrown away with abandon.

Reading my words it would appear that I am advocating a stretching and contracting of tempo so exaggerated as to pull the music out of shape, but as I have said many times before, these are fluctuations so minute in reality that the listener is unaware of them; only the performers know, and if they are making their *rubato* obvious they are over-doing it and deserve to be censured.

The rhythm is under constant control and the singer might be helped in this respect by ensuring that his dotted quavers (8, 15) are given their full value almost to the point of prolongation whenever they occur— and I can find ten of them in this short song in the vocal line alone. There are in the pianoforte interludes, half a dozen instances of this particular rhythmic shape; the pianist must not snatch his hand away from the dotted quaver whether it be in bass or treble,

Ex.4

but must hurry the semiquavers in the second half of the bar (as the singer did in 8 and 15) and counteract by making his energetic chords (18) uncompromising.

As if to exemplify the madly high spirits of the man 'Lustig in die Welt hinein' etc. is put into the major; the word 'Lustig' should be relished with the sibilant thrown out aggressively. 'Sind wir selber Götter', fierce and defiant is repeated, and the question arises, should the singer be allowed some special dispensation on his top note?

Ex.5

sind wir sel-ber Göt - ter!

I only pose this question knowing how tempting it is in a song of such rapid declamation to make the rafters ring with the one and only high note that exists. No concession is to be made. We want to hear the tone on this top G, but any lingering on it would be artificial, would betray a complacent calculation out of keeping with the character of the song. In any case a high G of itself is no reason for making an undue fuss. Schubert perhaps felt this; he originally had *Muth* in A minor but a merciful second thought prompted him to transpose it down one tone— greatly to the relief of baritones.

XXIII. DIE NEBENSONNEN

'THREE SUNS shine on me through the mist, long I gazed at them but
they seemed reluctant to leave me. Suns of the mist you are not mine,
go shine for other men. Once indeed I had three suns, but two, the best
of them, sank. When the third sets I shall be in darkness, welcome
darkness.'

I believe the phenomenon of three suns can be explained scientifically,
but here it would seem to be allegorical. The distinguished musicologist
A. H. Fox-Strangways suggested that Faith, Hope and Life are repre-
sented—a poetic conclusion and in the context of the cycle an acceptable
one. Most certainly the suns of Faith and Hope exist no more for our
afflicted wanderer, all that is left to him is Life and that is a stuff he
would readily do without.

The mood of the song is mournful, an extreme contrast and reaction
to the wildness of *Muth*.

To some extent the block harmony is reminiscent of *Das Wirtshaus*
and I have heard the two songs performed as if they were akin. Let
me say at once that the church-yard scene, the decorous tone of voice,
the subdued organ-like accompaniment of *Das Wirtshaus* bear no
relation whatsoever to *Die Nebensonnen*. The two are as different as
night is from day.

The same pattern is used continuously; even the short and vital link
modulating from the tonic to the minor third C major (16–19) is a
variation of it. It is a pattern using only four notes, all within the span
of a fourth.

Into these bare bones Schubert has breathed life.

Sometimes in an attempt to qualify dynamics, allusion is made to a
Brahms *piano* or *pianissimo* or to a Chopin *p* or *pp*, the inference being
that the latter in consistence, is delicate and ephemeral as opposed to
the former's strength and solidity. (This is only a generalization and is
not to say that Brahms was incapable of elegance or Chopin of force.)

Performers would be advised to have a Brahms quality of *piano* in mind when performing *Die Nebensonnen*. I recommend this for considerations which will be made clear later, but one reason is that the accompaniment has a suggestion of brass about it—the French horn let us say—and is set in the most sonorous register of the instrument, never in fact leaving it.

Ex.1

It is impossible to do justice to that poetic turn in 3 if the player sticks rigidly to the beat, the turn must be given plenty of latitude.

Ex. 2

The tessitura of the vocal line, nearly always in the middle of the voice, lies gratefully for the singer. Were he to interpret the sign *pp* literally as an injunction to sing *mezza voce* it would belittle the music, it is sung with a carrying resonant tone which adds to the sadness of his message and makes it ring true.

In this example the semiquavers are important. Sometimes it is desirable to relieve passing notes of pressure, to pass lightly over them either to give wing to rhythmic movement or to focus attention on the high point of a phrase, here the passing notes or semiquavers are no weaker than their neighbours.

There should be no mistaking the *forte* at 10.

In the example above (2) the pianoforte chord in 7 and 12 is played against the triplet, a proceeding which is reversed in the minor section

Ex. 3

where it is the voice's turn to pay no regard to the triplet. Each step in this climb becomes more and more impassioned until the expansive *crescendo* in 19 leads to an imposing climax of tragic grandeur. The singer should make the most of it, it is his last chance before the cycle ends to sing with deep and telling sonority.

Ex. 4

After the *diminuendo* in 23, the spirit which has pervaded the song droops and one is prepared for it by the interlude.

Ex. 5

This is played with infinite sympathy, as *legato* as possible, and with a slight hesitation before the dominant chord in 25.

'When the third sun sets I shall be in welcome darkness.' With these sad words the song resumes its now familiar pattern in the tonic key; naturally it is softly done—this is the song's quietest moment—but not so subdued as to be out of character with the quality of tone the singer has been using. Never for a moment must the numbness that is going to overwhelm the wanderer in the final song be anticipated; here in *Die Nebensonnen* he makes his final compelling outcry.

XXIV. DER LEIERMANN

NO MATTER how many years you have known *Der Leiermann* or how often you have thought about and rehearsed it, the song always holds you. It is a marvel and a supreme example of Schubert's magic in that while recognizing its greatness we are unable to explain the why or wherefore. It looks commonplace on paper, has invariable two-bar phrases, never modulates and hardly ever rises above a *pianissimo* level, surely the epitome of and ideal recipe for monotony and yet when sung it grips your heart and mind from first note to last and moves you to tears. The musician living with this song throughout his life envies the young student who has yet to experience the wonder of it.

Richard Capell truly asserted 'Given a thousand guesses, no one would have said that the last song would be at all like this'.

For so long, the wanderer has sought forgetfulness. Was he destined to find it by following the example of the more youthful journeyman miller? Wilhelm Müller had the inspiration to put the organ-grinder in his path. After the rages, illusions, miseries, the hopeless dreams of dead departed days, it remains for the organ-grinder, the only living being he has noticed on the wintry pilgrimage, to teach our friend some small measure of tranquillity; it is he who brings down the final curtain and enables the lone actor in the cycle to make his exit with a new found courage.

'Beyond the village stands an organ-grinder, turning out his tunes with frozen fingers, shuffling to and fro on the ice with bare feet, not a single penny on his little tray. No one seems to hear or heed him, only the dogs snarl at his heels, but this troubles him little—come what may he goes on grinding out his tunes—and the drone goes on and on.

'Wonderful old fellow, let me come with you. Will you grind out your music to my sad songs??'

The centre of the picture is the ragged old vagrant, he always holds the eye; the ear is held by the wheezy tune and pedal-point fifth of the instrument he plays. This drone rivets the singer's attention in the eight introductory bars, after which he catches sight of the man. The singer is a spectator of the scene and although we overhear his words he is actually soliloquising, his tone invariably subdued. He does not impersonate the organ-grinder but is so fascinated that his vocal timbre is influenced by the aspect of the old man and in consequence his voice is unrecognizable as the voice heard in *Die Nebensonnen*.

Recitative in style, at every utterance of the voice the accompaniment is moveless.

The pianist is the organ-grinder or rather the pianoforte is the organ. There is no more expression in this accompaniment than there would be in the miserable instrument the pianoforte is representing. It is mechanical.

Ex.1

What then of the stresses and semiquaver rests to be noticed whenever the organ is played?

My notion of this organ is of a cumbersome box with a handle at the side, from its base a wooden prop hangs and rests on the ground to take its weight, a leather strap round the neck of the player keeps the thing stable. The whole contraption is lifted up for a second—so that the man can take a step—and then lowered; this is the reason for the short silences in the treble and for the slight jolt as the machine is raised and stumped down—'Steht ihm nimmer still'. The bass predominates and its incessant droning is heard above the paltry tune and through those semiquaver rests. Hardly any sustaining pedal is used;—(save to link the bass fifths together) especially in the semiquaver rests there must be no overtones in the treble—the gap in the tune should be apparent.

The argument that the vocal line should be as mechanical as the pianoforte can be ruled out at once, it is the accompaniment that is the machine, not the singer; for the latter to overload his phrases with expressive nuances would be equally wrong and betray misunderstanding. The singer's role needs deep thought; although his emotion is restrained, what he says stands out in extreme contrast to the mindless accompaniment. He has to steer his course between the Scylla of understatement and the Charybdis of over-emphasis. As I said earlier the voice is always subdued, tone should be colourless—the quality of the violin or violoncello when played *non vibrato*—but the notes are clearly sung. Clarity of enunciation and mastery of speech rhythm combine to make the spasmodic utterances spell-binding. Speech rhythm, yes. Words here are sung as naturally as they would be if spoken.

The little airs in Ex. 2 and 3 are each repeated four times and are vivified solely by elasticity of declamation.

Ex. 2

Bars 9-10 Drü-ben hin-term Dor-fe   steht ein Lei-er - mann,
Bar   13   star-ren Fin-gern
Bar   35   die Hun-de knur-ren

Bar 9 can be sung as written, it has the exact note values of speech rhythm though it would be natural to stress 'Dorfe' a little; on the other hand 10 is a longer bar, 'ein Leiermann' is the pivot on which everything depends and needs more time. In 13 it is 'starren Fingern' where imagination is gripped; again it deserves time and emphasis—but not more volume. ('Barfuss auf dem Eise' Example 3 follows immediately and is given similar bite.) All the remaining utterances 'dreht er was er kann'—'wankt er hin und her'—'und sein kleiner Teller bleibt ihm immer leer' etc. are as colourless and empty as the little tray. Only at 35 'die Hunde knurren' the singer will be roused to give some thrust to 'knurren' (the rolling 'r's') so as to reflect the snarling; if more tone were needed to accomplish this it would be condoned.

Bars 17-18   Bar – fuß auf dem Ei – se wankt er hin und her,
Bars 21-22   und sein klei-ner Tel-ler bleibt ihm im-mer leer.

The above alternates with Ex. 2; it is given here to warn the singer to resist the temptation to make a *crescendo* up to the high E—even on the frigid 'Barfuss'. Always the colour is grey and old above the expressionless unceasing drone of the organ.

World weariness is the message, and the art of the singer makes it a pallid one. The composer would not thank him for giving every quaver and every crotchet its exact value (only the accompaniment is responsible for rhythmical exactitude and is inevitably, intentionally monotonous) and this freedom makes it possible for him to communicate the thoughts of the watching man so naturally.

At the words 'Wunderlicher Alter' a shaft of light brightens the gloom, the cold band clutching the broken man's heart for so long melts in a wave of warmth. He no longer regards the old man with detachment; within him there stirs an affection, a feeling of kinship for one who continues to endure life's buffetings and slights with such sublime indifference. It is yet another of Schubert's life enhancing inspirations. What a responsibility for the singer!

Wun-der-li-cher Al-ter,   soll ich mit dir gehn?

Willst zu mei-nen Lie-dern dei-ne Lei-er drehn?

The pianoforte accents are to be construed as exhalations, heartfelt sighs, and they help the singer's 'Wunderlicher'. The first syllable of 'Wunderlicher'—even before we have heard the complete word—contains a world of meaning, the voice now vibrates with warmth and humanity.

Has it been noticed that there are no expression marks? Another Lieder writer, anxious to guide us, might have inserted 'Sehr aus—drücksvoll' or 'Mit tiefer Empfindung', instructions which in this instance would be redundant and misleading, for the deep emotion in the man's heart is still restrained, he is still talking to himself. When he says 'soll ich mit dir gehn?' he is not calling aloud to the organ-grinder.

Later the innate hope expressed in 'Willst du meinen Liedern deine Leier drehn?' demands an eager spirit from the singer and a *crescendo* is the natural outcome, but this must, simply must, be kept within bounds. He is still the same soliliquiser who started the song, it would be ruinous to step out of character and suddenly, from nowhere, produce a ringing tone.

Ex. 5

The *forte* in this postlude is inadmissible so far as I am concerned. I cannot see how this miserable organ could be capable of loudening in this way, indeed its very ineptitude makes bar 58 the more poignant, the more pitiful.

I recommend an extended *fermata* on the dominant chord in 60 before sinking into the almost inaudible tonic. It is the long and final cadence to a very great work.

SCHWANENGESANG

I. LIEBESBOTSCHAFT

OF ALL Schubert's rippling streams—*Wohin, Die Forelle, Auf dem Wasser zu singen, Der Jüngling an der Quelle* and many more joyous burblings besides, it is *Liebesbotschaft* that is his final cloudless aquarelle. It bubbles and gushes inexhaustibly bearing in an eternal springtime the message of the young lover to his mistress. It is a charming conceit—implausible but refreshing.

The lover asks the rushing brook, so silvery and clear, to take his loving greetings to the darling of his heart; 'The flowers in her garden' he says—'her glowing roses, refresh them with your cool waters and when on your bank she wanders lost in sad loneliness comfort her by saying her beloved will soon return. Finally when the sun sets, rock that dear maid to sleep with your drowsy murmur, whispering love to her.'

Ziemlich langsam, Schubert's injunction, seems to belie the description of joyousness that I have given it, but the notes in the pianoforte's treble are not semiquavers they are demisemiquavers; moreover there are two beats to the bar (definitely not four) and these are slow beats—approximately $\boldsymbol{\delta} = 56$. It will be found that this tempo is felicitous; the stream flows happily but without agitation and the player is able to play with ease and relaxation. (In the original key of G major the fingers seem to fall naturally into place and cope effortlessly with the 'double-stopping'. In E major or E flat it is another story; these transpositions entail care and preparation to maintain evenness and to circumvent jarring or fuss.) A singer for whom I had great esteem was so impressed by the mark *langsam* that she refused to sing it at my tempo and we performed the song twice as slowly as the speed I advocate, with the result that the rippling stream became sluggish.

Ex.1

A uniform *piano* obtains here—no rises and falls (it is much easier to make a *crescendo* up to the first beats of 2 and 4 but better to avoid it if possible) and the passing G sharp in 3 is to be heard. No slowing down is made in 5 before the voice's entry.

'Silbern und hell' is the singer's guide, his tone is always light in weight and light in texture; his smoothness of line contrasts with the chuckling movement of the pianoforte. Words ('Rauschendes Bächlein so silbern'—'eilst zur Geliebten'—'die Grüsse des Fernen') must be enjoyed for their own sake, they are projected with zeal without disturbing the over-riding *piano*. Clear articulation of the sibilants brings the voice forward and helps to produce bright tone so essential in this song. The singer is always conscious of the murmuring waters which seem to respond to his invocation in bars 8 and 11

where the pianist allows the tenor voice to sing eagerly.

Several opportunities occur for the singer to charm us by his sensitive musicianship:

Ex. 3

brin-ge die Grü-ße des Fer - nen ihr zu.

the big leap on 'Grüsse' is only wide for the performer but not for the listener who should not know that a technical feat is accomplished since it has been done with smoothness and without a *crescendo* on to the high G (anybody could do it with a *crescendo*). The little passage is all *piano* and it is made even more graceful if the two top notes are allowed a little play before arriving gently on 'Fernen'.

Ex.4

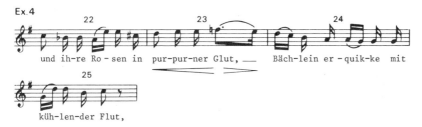

und ih-re Ro - sen in pur-pur-ner Glut, ⎯ Bäch-lein er -quik-ke mit

küh-len-der Flut,

The above comes twice and the comma after 'Glut' is a trap for the unwary singer who feels the punctuation mark permits him to take a breath, this kills the flow of the music: everything stands still while the tank is being refuelled. There must be no waiting; in other words the four bars are taken in one breath.

Not for a moment would I suggest that the pianoforte supplies more than a background to this picture, but there are several features in the accompaniment—apart from the rippling treble—which should not be glossed over. We have seen in Ex. 2 how the pianoforte makes its response in those tiny interludes and this happens again and again where it actually echoes the singer.

Ex. 5   Ex. 6

mein Bo - te sei du;

The little *staccato* semiquavers in the base are fascinating and they become even more bubbly and amusing when Schubert turns them into fifths at 18 for four successive bars, a rhythmic pleasantry to be repeated in bars 32 and 36.

More tranquillity is suggested now by the *pianissimo* at the thought of the maiden wandering by the riverside and by the dreamy descent of the pianoforte bass

Ex. 7

Excitement mounts at 'tröste die Süsse mit freundlichen Blick, denn der Geliebte kehrt bald zurück' and the singer lets us hear his enthusiasm at the little outbursts—marked by Schubert—during these eight bars and culminating in

Ex. 8

after which he returns to his softest and most confidential tone for 'rock her to sleep with your drowsy murmur'. In fact he sings 'flustre ihr Träume der Liebe zu' (61, 62) to the same notes as bars 15 and 16 (Ex. 3) and it would be fatal if he made a boisterous *crescendo*.

At 59 the grace note is treated as an *acciaccatura*.

II. KRIEGERS AHNUNG

WHEN SCHUBERT in his youth was dealing with a text of operatic or cantata style he employed the *recitative-arioso* formula, we find it in his earliest songs *Hagars Klage*, *Des Mädchens Klage*, *Der Vatermöder* and many of those Lieder wherein he might be said to be practising his hand, feeling his way towards his eventual incomparable summit. But he never discarded the recitative idea altogether, in *Die schöne Müllerin* for instance it can be seen in *Feierabend* ('Und der Meister spricht zu allen') and in *Der Neugierige* ('Ja, heisst das eine Wörtchen') where recitative links one section with another (it would be a misconception to regard the description as disparaging for the link or recitative in *Der Neugierige* is the very essence of the song) and serves to prepare the listener and lead him to a change of scene and mood.

Kriegers Ahnung (Warrior's foreboding) is a series of sections each with its own unmistakable Schubertian finger print with much imposing music, but each unconnected; each initiated—apart from the majestic pianoforte introduction—with an unexpected abruptness whether its theme be fear, longing, excitement, tearfulness. The performers miss the coupling that a recitative affords between these parts, and in an attempt to relate one to the other it is suggested they agree to a tempo at the outset that will carry some homogeneity. Here is a metronome beat which can govern loosely the three different time signatures.

It may be observed I give myself a loophole by using the qualifying 'loosely', for truth to tell the time relationship between these movements cannot be exact, but singer and player do their best to give the three sections a semblance of affinity.

The scene of the slumbering encampment is portrayed in the first verse. Night has brought rest to all except to one soldier, who, fearful, consumed with passionate longing for his mistress, lies sleepless.

Ex.1

Save for the sudden *fp* in 4—the tossing of the wretched man in his blanket—it is all *pianissimo*, but it is a *pp* full of foreboding and the angular semiquavers, the sudden stops make a pattern that suggests apprehension. Tempo is strict.

Ex.2

Schubert's over-all mark is *pianissimo* but it is of Brahmsian vintage for the singer remembers he is playing the part of a man and a soldier at that, who is well acquainted with danger therefore nothing should be tentative in the singing—the tone full-bodied and manly.

Ex.3

Exactitude is imperative in such a phrase as this; 'Bang und schwer' it may be but it must not be ragged and to achieve unanimity of attack the singer shows consideration and lets his partner *see* what he is doing.

Verse two is as different from the first verse as it is possible to be: 'How often I have had sweet dreams close to her warm breast when she lay in my arms! How friendly the glow from the hearth.'

Ex. 4

For the time being the singer does well to thrust the masculine side of our hero to the background and give us light lyrical singing; no longer are there the convulsive stops and starts we had earlier, all is smooth. The *pianissimo* seen in some editions at bar 29 is not authentic: the pianoforte can be extremely quiet but the voice will have more scope for nuance if *mezzopiano* is the norm. These pleasant bars are repeated until we are brought back to an immediate awareness of our surroundings by

Ex. 5

'Here the flickering flame of the camp fire plays only on weapons, here the heart feels forsaken and tears fill my eyes'.

Tears or no tears, the singer must revert to the timbre of the opening verse, he cannot afford in 43, 44 to obey the *pianissimo*, his tone needs depth and weight to ride over the accompaniment which lies in a sonorous part of the instrument. 'Hier, wo die Flammen düstrer Schein' is projected with bitterness, in acute contrast to the previous 'Wie freundlich schien des Herdes Glut'. The pianist will be hard put to it to keep his C sharp octaves and repeated chords in the right hand from over resonance for they are not *staccato* and the sustaining pedal has to be used. From 44 to 47 it is the pianoforte bass which is to be heard.

The words 'der Wehmut Träne quillt' seem to signify that the passage

Ex.6

should be sung with pitiful expression but this would be wrong; in 50 and 53 'ganz allein' had its *fp* and here the sweep up to 'Wehmut' must be allowed its natural impetus with no lessening of tone in 58, 59. It would be a let down to treat this section too quietly, for the excitement of the triplets (Ex. 5) demands passionate response from the singer moreover it prepares the listener, to some extent, for the most agitated movement of the song which comes in a trice.

'Be strong, my heart, and prepare for battle. Soon I shall sleep so I bid my darling goodnight.'

Following immediately on the martial 'prepare for battle' the comfortable 'soon I shall sleep' is something of a *volte-face* especially when the warrior's fears and tears of the previous stanzas are considered, and

for this Rellstab is responsible; these muddled sentiments are taken by
Schubert in his stride.

Ex.7

The so-called 'unimportant' quavers on the third and sixth beats in the pianoforte are not to be neglected, they add to the disturbance under the treble's fierce semiquavers. (61–72)

'Nicht verlässt' is sung bravely, the speed and aggressive *crescendo* impel the singer to mount from the A flat to the F with a slide; no matter, the slide is not reprehensible and will prevent him from giving us 'ni-hicht'. 'Schlacht' is forcible to the very end of the note, the singer must not warn us of his impending *pianissimo* in 73 it is for the pianist in 71, 72 to pave the way for the soothing section but he does it by his steep *diminuendo* and with no slackening of speed.

This movement of 28 bars with its two discrepant halves is repeated.

Schubert brings the song to an end by re-introducing the scene of the sleeping camp with its nervous semiquavers, its unsettling silences, and thus can be said to have taken us full circle.

Ex. 8

There is no slackening of speed at 111 forestalling tempo 1. Bars 110 and 111 are still $\half. = 52$ and it is only on the second syllable of 'Herz-liebste' (112) that the slower pace of the first movement is suddenly resumed.

III. FRÜHLINGSSEHNSUCHT

'CARESSING BREEZES wafting fragrant flowery scents—rippling brooks, what have you done to my heart which longs to follow you—but whither? Why, golden sunshine, though your welcoming glance refreshes me do my eyes fill with tears? Why? Verdant forests, blossoms, swelling seeds reach up to this sunshine and are fulfilled. O, restless desires! Like the buds and blossoms I feel an urge that cannot be allayed, who will still my ardent longing? Only you, just you.'

To this expression of spring fever there are five verses, in strophic form, that fly like the wind and dance like a sunbeam. But that it is repetitive cannot be denied and it would be wise to take it at a cracking speed, say ♩ = 80 thinking in terms of one beat to the bar. Not one of the Master's most distinguished songs yet exhilarating to sing and play; the performers do their utmost to make their high spirits infectious.

In bars 3 to 6 the tenor voice's ascent catches the ear, at 5 the soprano joins in and takes over (7, 8); at 9 the alto voice bears the burden so that the effect is

Except for a few bars the triplet accompaniment persists—and always in the style of Ex. 1—always with the treble echoing and coming just after the singer's melody.

There is no reason to attempt to sing *legato*—only in the pianoforte bass (13, 14, 15, 16 etc.) is it so marked—the words trip off the tongue buoyantly. 'Säuselnde Lüfte', 'Grüssender Sonne spielendes Gold' have sibilants that should be relished, and there is no excuse for the labial 'Lüfte' 'blumiger Düfte' to be anything but refreshingly clear. All through the song, despite the rapidity of movement the consonants bring the voice forward—and they bounce the sound from note to note —the separate bows of the string player.

Ex.2

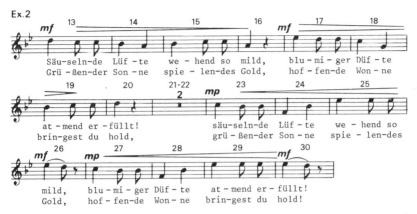

Säu-seln-de Lüf-te we-hend so mild, blu-mi-ger Düf-te
Grü-ßen-der Son-ne spie-len-des Gold, hof-fen-de Won-ne

at-mend er-füllt! säu-seln-de Lüf-te we-hend so
brin-gest du hold, grü-ßen-der Son-ne spie-len-des

mild, blu-mi-ger Düf-te at-mend er-füllt!
Gold, hof-fen-de Won-ne brin-gest du hold!

Distinctly four bar phrases, the rests in 16 and 26 are to be observed, but there is hardly time for breaths to be taken nor should they be necessary, in fact excitement is generated without them. I have indicated my liking for a falling from *mezzo forte* to *mezzopiano* in the first two phrases and a rising in the last two.

Only from 33 to 40

Ex.3

Wie haucht ihr mich won-nig be-grü-ßend an! wie habt ihr dem
Wie labt mich dein se-lig be-grü´ßen-des Bild! es lä-chelt am

po-chen-den Her-zen ge-tan?
tief-blau-en Him-mel so mild

should we feel a steady increase of tone from 'Wie haucht' to 'Herzen' the summit. It should be considered as a sweeping eight bar phrase contained in one span with the rest in 36 regarded only as a comma.

An eight bar passage comes again at 42 to 49

Ex.4

es möch-te euch fol gen auf luf-ti-ger Bahn, es möch te euch
und hat mir das Au ge mit Trä nen ge-füllt, und hat mir das

There is to be no suggestion of slowing down before the sudden arrest of movement on 'Wohin?' bars 50 and 52, the tempo remains ♩ = 80 for Schubert has stretched it out for us; at the voice's entry (58) the song becomes air-borne again.

In my essay on *Ungeduld* (*Die Schöne Müllerin*) I referred to the bass semiquaver as seen in bar 44 of *Frühlingssehnsucht* and gave my opinion that it should be played as a triplet to coincide with the pianist's treble and I have so marked it in example 4.

Second, third and fourth verses are like unto the above but the final verse is in the minor with an excursion to D flat major from which Schubert returns to the tonic with disarming nonchalance.

A good tenor will enjoy the *tessitura* of his part throughout, and he has a ringing top A towards the end but he takes it without pausing in his flight. This direction also obtains in the closing bars of the postlude, made with no pedestrian *rallentando*.

Once again I refer the reader to Eric Blom's wise counsel on the subject of repeats which I quoted in *Thränenregen* (*Die Schöne Müllerin*). Backed by the authority of this musician's profound scholarship I would put a case for the performers not making the *da capo*; proceeding, that is to say, from the second direct to the fifth verse. This is the only instance in all the songs embraced in this book where I make such a suggestion. In all fairness I must add I have never performed the cut in practice, perhaps I was lucky in partnering singers who held my eager interest from first note to last.

IV. STÄNDCHEN

If RELLSTAB was cavalierly treated by the suggested cuts in *Frühlings-sehnsucht*, credit is his for providing a lyric which Schubert has fashioned into one of the world's most famous songs, indeed it is so celebrated and popular (painfully popular), subjected to such ill-treatment that one is apt to forget how eloquent it can be.

'Hear my songs, sweetheart, and come down to me, let us listen together to the nightingales singing for they know love's smart, they know the night quivers with desire. Come my darling, come and bring joy to my heart.'

Justice cannot be done to Schubert without giving the lovely melody some thought. Obviously it must be smooth, equally obviously 'Leise flehen' demands a mellifluous quality of voice. What of the shape? Let us take the bare bones of the tune.

The phrase is dull and lifeless, but the missing triplet transforms it

There is Schubert—there is radiance. The *melisma* is the life-blood of the music and on it the singer bestows tender care. Each note is equal in time—not ♪♫♩. or ♫♪♩.—and equal in weight, more, the first beat carrying the precious cargo is the longest beat in the bar and is the personification of earnest pleading banishing triviality and the fatuous smile. Musical metre takes precedence over verbal in so far as the triplets are stretched—not because they happen to be on the first beat of the bar, but to give them eloquent shape. These opening passages are *pianissimo*—not one note is given more tone than another so that the listener is spared such common-place treatment as

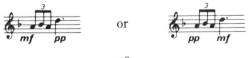   or

which give painful evidence of bad musicianship. The rest in 6 does not necessarily enjoin a breath.

Surely the high point emotionally is the urgent 'Liebchen, komm zu mir' (this is what it is all about) and the singer lets us know this by an added intensity, by an extra vibration; he will make it significant if he observes the comma after 'hernieder', breaking for a moment the flow of sound—to do it in one breath would be preferable but not essential, it is the break which matters.

From the *staccato* marking in the introduction it is evident that Schubert wanted a guitar-like accompaniment. After the strings of the guitar are plucked the tone lingers momentarily, the pianoforte's brisk *staccato* by comparison is too blunt and dry, the player therefore aims at a *pizzicato* quality of sound and should not snatch his fingers too sharply off the keys. Sustaining pedal is not wanted in the first seven bars, only at 8 is it needed with the lightest pressure; it is certainly required at 9, 10 where the treble echoes the vocal phrase—an echo with a soft singing tone, as distinct from an anaemic tinkling, and with the triplet shaped as was the singer's. The *crescendo* I have inserted is *pochissimo* and hardly to be noticed.

Does Schubert suspect we shall have made a slight increase of tone at 17, 18? This perhaps explains the *pianissimo* at 19.

It is as if the serenader suddenly restrains his excitement. The last syllable of 'rauschen' is sometimes robbed by a snatched breath or by impatience to get up to the grace notes in 19 and if a breath is necessary this can be an ungainly corner disturbing to the smoothness of line. The remedy—and here the vigilant pianist can be helpful—is to slow down a little so that the breath can be taken with composure. Bars 25, 51, 57 are similar.

'Fürchte, Holde, nicht' (Fear not) must of necessity be *forte* as marked

and the pianist forgets the guitar and gives the voice the support it needs; the *forte* too is anticipated by a *crescendo* on the last three quavers of 26 for without it we should get a sudden volley of sound which, following the *pianissimo*, would be calculated to frighten any maiden out of her wits. No singer would be blamed for not hastening off his top G and indeed a time stress is there.

The interlude of eight bars, alternating with passion and tenderness, shows clearly whether the pianist is living in the song or not, his tone rings with as much fervour as his partner's.

It is a poetic passage, and again richness of colour such as the pianoforte can supply is wanted. The first four bars are an uninhibited *mezzo
forte* and the last four *pianissimo*, the bridge between these is the third
beat of 32 which has a *subito pp*. This up beat if lingered on kindles an
affectionate suspense before it merges with melting effect into the major
chord of 33. The soprano and alto voices sing as a duo throughout this
interlude.

Largely the first two verses can be summed up as subdued pleading,
but in the last verse the fire that consumes the lover cannot be held in
check.

Ex. 5

From 61 there is a quickening of tempo, slight but immediate, the
urgency of the words, the energetic rhythm of the vocal line demand it.
Of the third beats that are stressed from 61 to 64 the most vital are
'höre mich' (63)—much more insistent than supplicatory—and the
pianoforte's third beat of 64 since it portends the climax at 65.

'Bebend harr ich dir entgegen' (trembling I await you) seems at face value the sentiment of a timorous lover but it is the cry of a love-sick swain who trembles with passion whose blood surges hotly through his veins. The energy of the voice's rising figure with the pianoforte in pursuit (61, 62) the quickened pace, the thrilling modulating bar into B minor with that ringing F sharp on 'Bebend' all conspire to make this the most potent moment of the song; to justify it I recommend the singer to make a short *fermata* on his huge F sharp and the pianist to ignore his *diminuendo* in that same bar.

I would not quarrel with the notion that 71 'Komm beglükke mich' (come, bring joy to my heart) with its top G is the climax but it would not be my choice.

Ex. 6

After the *forte* in 67 a *diminuendo* in the pianoforte prepares for the singer's soft entreaty in 69. Again for the big vocal phrase in 71 there should be a swelling of tone on the last three quavers of the accompaniment in 70, a *subito forte* would be the reverse of persuasive.

The passion of 'beglükke mich' is sustained until 74 and then the singer has 'room' for his *diminuendo*, it is a mistake to start softening too soon; in pursuance of this the pianoforte's stressed octave F natural should be *forte*. Likewise the *pianissimo* in the postlude renders the possibility of a *decrescendo* impracticable; by substituting a *piano* for the *pianissimo* the player will be enabled to allow his tone to die away gently.

This accompaniment hardly presents unreasonable difficulties technically, even so the player should be on his guard, he makes sure that the almost unnoticed *pizzicato* chords are synchronized. This is what can happen in *Ständchen* and *Ave Maria* and many other Schubert piano parts through sheer carelessness.

It is bad playing, un-selfcritical listening. One should never be too sure of oneself.

V. AUFENTHALT

'RAGING TORRENT, roaring forest, stubborn rocks you are my resting place. Fury of wind, beating wave on wave, you are like my tears—unceasing. The tree tops swaying and the breaking branches match my heart. My agony is immovable as the rocks, so howl on, storm! Roar river!'

As the wanderer in *Der Stürmische Morgen* and *Mut* seemed to find a perverse consolation in the violence of the elements, so the sufferer in *Aufenthalt* feels the turmoil in his heart reflected in the storm-tossed trees, sees himself as the rock for ever enduring the beating of the waters, for ever suffering under their lash.

There is a conflict too in the rhythmical pattern of the music, continually we have triplet-quavers moving against quavers-in-pairs, and fours opposing triplets.

Ex.1

The quavers in the bass 2, 3, 4 (the rocks) are impervious to the treble triplets (the restless waters)—of this there can be no question; but what about 7, 8, 10, 12? Should the semiquaver in these bars lose its identity and succumb to the triplet? Would that carry out Schubert's instruction 'Kräftig' (robust)? Should the rock become malleable in this wise?

Ex. 2

The mere look of this is revolting. No, the semiquaver always comes after the triplet, defiantly, the singer sets the pattern with his first phrase.

'Nicht zu geschwind' is about ♩ = 88 and the pianist will find this quite quick enough by the time he has reached the final bar. It is his bass which predominates, it answers the voice in 8–9, 16–17, 18–19; the beating treble chords supply the motive power and are allowed plenty of sustaining pedal.

Rauschender—brausender—starrender like the English 'turbulent'—

'blustering'—'obdurate' have their stress on the first syllable and I am not suggesting this rule should be thrown overboard, but I do like to hear, in the context of this song, the third syllable of these words ejaculated fiercely—shaken off savagely whether it comes on a 'weak' semiquaver or not; it gives the listener a jolt. (These words of course, could not be spoken in this way for the stress would be only on the first syllable, but in singing we are allowed this license. The effect is rude and arresting.)

The four bar phrase 11 to 14 (as distinct from the two bar phrases) should be carried off with an impressive sweep.

Ex. 3

Wie sich die Wel-le an Wel - le reiht,

This example is for the attention of the pianist, for two reasons. There are many notes in the vocal line that lie below the stave and they are not too comfortable for some tenors, I therefore beg the player, when they are encountered to show his partner a little mercy.

Aufenthalt, literally translated as 'Resting Place', hardly lives up to its title in the pianist's estimation, for its repeated octaves and chords persist without a point of rest throughout the song's 141 bars and can be tiring to the wrist—though not to be compared in this respect with *Erlkönig* or *Auf der Bruck*. Nevertheless there are opportunities for the right hand to 'take it easy' if the player wishes to take advantage of them. It will be seen in Ex. 3 that I have transferred the B's in the treble clef —bars 25, 26, 28, 30 to the bass for the left hand to be responsible; this process can be applied elsewhere.

Ex. 4

flie-ßen die Trä-nen mir e - wig er-neut,   flie - ßen die Trä -
    cresc
- - nen   mir   e - wig,   e - wig er-neut,   flie-ßen die

Trä—nen mir e - wig er —neut.

With ever lengthening intervals bars 31 to 34 are an extension of 27 to 30. From the depths of 'die Welle' in 28 to 'fliessen die Tränen' is a long and laborious course and it should not be made to sound easy— we must be aware that effort is necessary; there is a mounting *crescendo* towards the climax in 44—the *diminuendo* marked in 37, 38 is *en passant* and does not detract from the over-all build up of tone. The singer sees to it that his even quavers are stubbornly distinct from his dotted quavers.

The central section of some 22 bars is deceptive; we are apt to imagine because it is in the relative major—is marked *piano*—has the accompaniment moving mostly in unison with the voice—that a more temperate mood prevails. This is not so, the vocal line still rises and falls energetically in pitch and with the repetition of 'Hoch in der Kronen' etc. is as indomitable as ever.

These considerations together with the cutting E flat on 72 dispel any thought of moderation in intensity.

Ex.5

hoch in den Kro - nen   wo - gend sich's regt, so   un - auf - hör-lich mein

Her - ze schlägt, so   un - auf - hör-lich mein Her   -   -   ze schlägt.

Each note in 75 although marked *legato* must have a vigour of its own and it would be a pitiful sign of weakness to make a *diminuendo* on the *melisma*: this is confirmed by the ruthless and immediate upsurge of the pianoforte in the interlude.

Ex.6

'My agony is as permanent as the rocks' has the motif we saw in 27 to 47 (Ex. 3 and 4) before we are brought back to a repetition of the opening subject (Ex. 1). This is interrupted dramatically when, with a stride, we go from E minor to C minor—this is the crucial point.

Ex.7

How rare for Schubert to have *fortississimo* in his score (the *ff* seen in most editions is incorrect) and he plainly wanted the singer to give all his worth in this tremendous moment. The pianoforte bass in 124 should indeed be precise but 125 and 126 can be stretched by the player to allow his partner glory. This resounding top note has no *diminuendo*, only the pianoforte diminishes in tone in anticipation of the octave drop of the voice in 127.

The *tessitura* of *Aufenthalt* lies uncomfortably high for a baritone voice. This song is not spoiled by being transposed down to D minor, in fact I venture to suggest that its darker deeper colour is more suitable than the original.

VI. IN DER FERNE

THE FUGITIVE forsaking friends and homeland, consumed with hatred for his fellow-men, doomed to a life of loneliness, asks wave and wind to carry to her who broke his heart, tidings of his miserable lot.

We cannot think of another Lieder writer who would have attempted to set such a poem—of which the above is the gist—to music, for it has little meaning, much verbosity and amounts to a lugubrious jingle. Capell suggests that the verses might have intrigued Schubert by their dancing rhymes. The problem of fashioning a song out of this material appears to be insurmountable but Schubert did not recognize the existence of any problems. I find myself studying the score of *In der Ferne* away from the pianoforte and the music looks dull and monotonous but when I hear it performed my feelings are stirred. So often, on the contrary, a piece of music *looks* wonderful on paper but does not *come off* in performance. Schubert was able to speak to the heart—this was his secret.

The introduction gives a descriptive foretaste of the sombre mood of the first two verses.

Ex.1

Once again my contention that Schubert's *fp* and his > symbol carry a different implication is borne out in this example for on the first beats of bars 1 and 3 both signs come simultaneously; one sign clearly asks for a sharp *sforzando* while the other is a time stress with little or no dynamic connotation. Therefore the first beats in 1 and 3 are dwelt on in addition to the stab of tone, while the first beats of 2, 4 and 5 are merely prolonged a little. This slight check to the motion gives added ominousness to the bass semiquavers.

We find in this song more detailed instructions than Schubert is in the habit of giving and if the singer is able to carry them out the music becomes all the more impressive.

Ex. 2

A quiet breath is taken after every second bar to help the singer maintain the most even and *piano* tone, only at 17 with the modulation to B flat comes the *crescendo* followed by a *subito piano* at 21. (Very little fuss should be made by the pianist at 12, this interlude—faintly indicated—is parenthetical and the *fermata* is hardly to be noticed.)

Ex. 3

The succession of two bar phrases comes to an end and we have a four and then a five-bar passage which need concentrated handling and firm breath control. Only the slenderest increase of tone on 22 is made; 'auf ihren Wegen nach' is conceived as a descent and leads to the *pianissimo* of 25. Time is taken for the breath before 25 so that 'nach' although whispered is as long as it can be comfortably sustained. If the pianist hangs about before arriving at his tonic chord on 28 he will not be loved by his partner; he should not be detected hurrying his chords on 'Wegen' for the singer's convenience, but he does not delay.

A typical Schubertian embellishment is given to the vocal line in the second verse.

By comparison with Ex. 2 the above has a deeper fervour and asks for a more ample *crescendo* at 46. (Not one iota earlier than marked, the eloquence of the four bars preceding is spoiled if the *crescendo* is anticipated. Bars 42 to 45 must be *mezza voce*.) This inevitably makes 'Klage, verhallende' a bigger *forte* than the corresponding 'Freunde verlassenden' of verse 1 and so far as Rellstab is concerned this perhaps is a contradiction, but the soaring vocal line demands it.

Light breaks through in the third verse, fortunately repeated with variation when the thought of wave and wind prompts Schubert to shower us gently with his endearing triplets and semiquavers. Thematically it is the same but now is in the major.

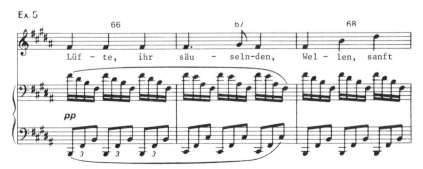

It is all *pianissimo* and the singer should obey the mood and adopt the colour that this very different lyrical writing calls for. One can say, perhaps, that Schubert conveniently evaded the earlier 'Mutterhaus hassenden, Freude verlassenden' mood in order to give us release from these ugly sentiments and to enchant us with two pages of beauty. It is sung coolly, smoothly, and without too much emotion; the music thus is allowed to speak for itself.

Against the voice's air a counter melody is heard in the accompaniment, contributing to the soothing rhythmic sway.

The one bar interludes of previous verses, which I resent (bars 12 and 41) now make a reappearance but in a different guise,

here however they are nostalgic echoes not interruptions, tenderly endorsing the voice's sentiments (91 and 94).

Only at the end of the song does the fugitive feel called upon to re-exert his obduracy.

It is a brave flourish and the *fortissimo* (rather surprising knowing Schubert's reticence) coming in the foreign key of C major is justified.

In my opinion, however, the *fortissimo* on the final chord is out of place, the climax came on 'Welt hinaus Ziehenden'—splendid top notes for the singer—and the last chord should be solid indeed but not a crash.

VII. ABSCHIED

Mässig geschwind is the indicated speed here for we are not galloping or even trotting (the cobblestones do not encourage such haste) but are moving forward at a brisk walking pace and the rider hardly bothers with the reins, he turns in his saddle and waves to his various girl friends (girls it would appear of great amiability and generosity) and smiles up at their windows. Love affairs in plenty he may have had but he does not leave his heart behind him, his farewell to the town wherein he has had so much pleasure is without regrets but rather with thoughts for 'To-morrow to fresh woods and pastures new'.

If we recall the rhythmic sound of a walking horse his hooves go 'clipper-clopper-clipper-clopper' so in this song each quaver represents a hoof beat and the approximate metronome mark becomes $\quarternote = 152$. The pianist may at first regard my suggested speed rather fast but if he considers my 'clipper-clopper' extravaganza he may see it is logical; he will undoubtedly find this a demanding accompaniment and is hereby warned that the spirit of the song largely depends on the buoyancy and vitality with which it is played.

Ex. 1a

Obviously the *staccato* in the treble is maintained from beginning to end of the song and it will be impossible to accomplish unless the wrist is loose, as relaxed as possible; if the player tightens he will be in trouble before the song is half over. It is then that the 'off-beat' lower harmonies are skimped and the figure seen in bars 2 and 6 of the introduction—and which recurs many times—will lose its resilience and become

Ex b

Always the bass quavers are detached.

It may be some consolation to the pianist if I remind him that it is to be lightly played; he is asked for a *pianissimo* at the voice's entry and beyond a small rise and fall here and there the accompaniment remains *pp* until the postlude. Very little sustaining pedal should be used though a slight touch with the singer's several *legato* passages (which I shall be indicating) would be acceptable. The pianoforte's volume at all times is below the voice's level.

So much for the willing horse—now for the rider. I picture him as a lusty young student full of the joy of life who in this happy town ('ihr freundlichen Mägdlein dort) has made many a conquest.

The treatment of the vocal line should be influenced by the pianoforte writing, it is not an instrumental *staccato* but it is certainly *non legato* in that each quaver has a separate energy, an energy not to be confused with strength, for the tone should be *piano* to the accompaniment's *pianissimo*.

Ex. 2

This energy is confined to the consonants; enthusiasm and youthful
zest are clearly made evident by the enunciation of 'du muntre, du
fröhliche Stadt' and by the scintillating sibilants in bars 13 to 17.

Surely a little sentiment is permitted at the beginning of the second
and fourth verses 'Farewell you trees, you garden so green' and 'Farewell dear sun, sink to your rest'.

The phrases beg for a smoother delivery—a shade of distinction from the
prevailing pointed utterance. It is a *legato* which embraces the 'Ade'
(39 and 89) and is anticipated by the pianoforte's sustaining pedal in
34 and 84. And it is at the close of verses two and four that the singer
may allow himself to 'look around' on the first syllable of 'Ade' and not
scuttle off the note in a matter of fact way.

Ex. 4

ihr freund-li-chen Mägd-lein   dort,   a - de! _____
du schim - mern-des Fen-ster-lein hell,   a - de! _____

I hardly like to suggest a holding back of tempo when the transition
to the minor followed by the modulation to C flat occurs

Ex. 5

but I ask the player to allow us to appreciate this charming change. I
draw his attention too, to the repeated notes in the bass which are heard
from time to time, they are like quiet taps on the *timpani* and are seen
in my Ex. 2 (bars 9, 11, 13), in Ex. 3 (bars 36, 38, 40) and they should
be discreetly relished.

I have marked the fingering I use, but this is a very individual affair
and what is good for me could prove a blight to another.

In many editions there is a repeat printed from bar 78 back to 29
and this is sometimes improperly ignored; in Mandyczewski the music
is written out in full and it should be performed this way.

VIII. DER ATLAS

THE FIRST of the great settings of Heine looks almost Wagnerian with
its thunders and lightnings, and in this little poem the poet exemplifies

Eric Sams's description of him as the myth maker. It is an awe-
inspiring picture—'I, miserable Atlas that I am, I carry on my shoulders
a whole world of sorrows; I bear the unbearable and my heart within me
will burst. Proud heart, you wanted endless happiness or endless
sadness and now you are abject'.

I find on listening to various recordings in which I participated that
the basic tempo of *Der Atlas* is roughly $\quad = 80$ (not to be rigidly
maintained) and this seems to live up to the *Etwas geschwind* instruction,

but on reflection I am of the opinion that this may be a thought too fast.
Those octaves in the bass are—or should be—an impediment so that
when the giant lifts up his voice he should feel the weight of those
octaves dragging him back. Again and again as in the fall on to the F
sharp (2 and 3) it is shewn that progress is unsteady—it is a stagger.
Every bar gives evidence of struggle and strain. Sustaining pedal must
be used in plenty but it must not trespass on the rests which come so
often on the third beat; these panting rests give added weight to the
cruel lurch that follows.

The vocal line and pianoforte bass move together with rhythmic exactitude and it is vital that the singer allows his partner to *see* what he is doing. If, standing in the bend of the pianoforte, the singer turns his face in the direction of the pianist there will be every chance of unanimity on the short anacrusis which comes in most bars in this section. The tempo as I have hinted is not mechanically rigid for the word 'Atlas' has been given more burden with its two ponderous beats than 'unglückselger'; the very word 'Atlas' is a picture in itself. Strong tone is needed; the *diminuendi* in 6 and 8 are not for the singer; these should be observed by the pianist and were inserted perhaps to give the voice some advantage over the rumblings in the accompaniment. Atlas himself may be near to breaking point but the singer, if he wishes to convey the terror of the scene, maintains his *forte* until 14 which marks the end of Schubert's first section. At this point we are only half way through Heine's first verse, the remainder being contained in five bars of singing which act as a link between two musical ideas; but my expression 'link' gives a false idea of the magnitude of this arduous ascent from the key of G minor to B major.

Ex.3

ich tra - ge Un-er-träg-li-ches, und bre-chen will mir das Herz im

Lei - - be.

Every step up is the embodiment of herculean effort marked by a loudening of tone and in bar 18 each stride is made with more and more labour—the semiquavers 'mir das' move with leaden feet—until we come to the climax. Three times in the song *fff* is demanded and is authentic; it is not an ordinary *fortissimo*, and when it comes (19, 38, 50) the preceding bar in each case is long drawn out so that the travail involved in reaching the summit is not belittled.

Ex.4

Du stol-zes Herz, du

We see now that the texture of the music undergoes a complete change.

No sustaining pedal is used at all and the sharp throbs in the pianoforte bass stand out by being followed by the *piano subito*.

It is imperative that the pace be held back on a firm rein; the phrases are short with panting utterance up to 28 and lose their meaning if hurried, moreover this steadying of pace will allow time to bring the semiquavers *after* the pianoforte's triplet—on no account should semiquaver and triplet synchronize; the effect is of breathless suspense.

Hitherto the shape of the vocal line—the jolting rhythm at the beginning, followed by the breathlessness of 'Du stolzes Herz' etc.—has not asked for *legato* singing but now quite suddenly a stream of steady tone is wanted on 'unendlich glücklich'; the awful word 'unendlich' is repeated thrice and given full measure. The *legato* indications in the above example are mine.

The second climax

Ex. 5

does not give the singer a resounding top note but evidently Schubert wanted 'elend' to be the culmination. 'Jetzo bist du' is the preparation for this high point and the tempo is held back with remorseless control, the three quavers in 37 are defiant of the accompanying triplets.

A similar treatment is given to the last of the great outbursts

Ex.6

and 'Schmerzen' must be allowed a slight *fermata*.

In each of these spasms 'Leibe' (19) 'elend' (38) 'tragen' (51) the singer does not make a conscious *diminuendo* onto the second syllable—his tone will inevitably decrease being lower in the stave but he tries to make the listener feel he is still maintaining his *fortissississimo*.

The pianist brings the song to an end with a huge *crescendo* on the penultimate bar, and for convenience's sake makes a slight comma before arriving with a fearful crash on the last chord.

I had second thoughts, it may be recalled, over the speed of this song and it is not only on the question of speed that I have changed my views.

In 1953 a book appeared entitled *Singer and Accompanist* (Eyre Methuen Ltd) in which I discussed the singing and playing of fifty songs, *Der Atlas* being one of them. I wrote these words for the accompanist's benefit 'Do not allow the demisemiquavers in your right hand to lapse into an uncontrollable *tremolo* for this will rob the rhythm of tightness'. I do not agree now with what I said, for the 'tightness of rhythm' I was—and am—so keen to preserve depends entirely on the pianoforte bass. The violent tremors in the treble of sections one and three are written as eight notes to the beat but if the player can possibly shake ten or more out of his sleeve instead of eight it is all to the good. Schubert rarely if ever used the term *tremolo* but that in fact is the effect of this shuddering figure.

Returning to bar 55, the pianist will find it possible to stretch this bar without the right hand slowing down if he thinks of it as a *tremolo* and this protraction gives his *crescendo* much more scope.

Concerning Schubert's *fortissimo* it is curious that throughout the two Müller Cycles—even in *Eifersucht und Stolz*, *Stürmische Morgen*, *Mut*—not once is *fff* demanded, yet in *Schwanengesang* the sign appears in *Aufenthalt*, *Der Atlas*, and *Der Doppelgänger* with some profusion.

IX. IHR BILD

HUMBERT WOLFE in his 'Selected Lyrics of Heine' (The Bodley Head) compares Heinrich Heine to the English poet A. E. Housman—'The facile romanticism of the early nineteenth century matched against the facile despair of the late nineteenth . . . the passing of love matched with a lament for the passing of youth'. Simplicity and concentration of language, melodramatic dolour, lyrical and rhythmic cadence of romantic verse, the occasional drop of irony were ingredients that combined to make each poet all that could be desired to a song com-

poser. *Ihr Bild* (Her picture) might easily have been plucked from the
'Dichterliebe' so Schumannesque is the style; 'Ich hab im Traum
geweinet' is its twin.

'In my dreams I stood before her portrait and the beloved features
seemed to awaken to life, a sweet smile played on her lips, tears seemed
to glisten in her eyes. Tears, too, flowed down my cheeks. Oh; I
cannot believe that I have lost you.'

Ex.1

Though marked *Langsam* it is evident by the *Alla breve* sign that
Schubert did not want the tempo to drag; the pulse beat is never four
to the bar. 'Dunkeln Träumen' (dark dreams) are the words that
influence the singer not only in this passage but right through the song
until his last phrase, until the moment he says 'I cannot believe I have
lost you'. It is only in his imagination that the countenance of the dear
one smiles and sheds tears, the vocal line therefore must be unsub-
stantial, a thin stream of sound which, none the less, is smooth.

A breath after 'Träumen' is advisable.

Ex. 2

Parallel nuances match the rises and falls in the vocal line, but these are only slight; in the above, for instance, it would be illogical to make too conspicuous a swelling on to the word 'heimlich'. We listeners should not be allowed to know that a breath is taken after 'Antlitz', a rest is marked and the singer takes advantage of it but he sings mentally *through* the rest.

But a long phrase comes:

Ex. 3

and is contained in one breath. It is *pianissimo* except for the magical 'Lächeln' which lights up the gloom for a fleeting moment, it is a passage of infinite tenderness, with the *alto* voice in the accompaniment (17) lending its warmth.

The opening air is heard again at the start of the last verse and is similarly phrased with a breath after 'flossen' (26).

Finally the bitter realization of his cruel lot rouses the dreamer and a passionate cry is wrenched from his lips,

Ex. 4

it is charged with unaffected but deeply felt emotion; the singer no longer holds his feelings in check as he climbs with mounting tone to 'dass ich dich' and then makes 'Verloren hab' fade despairingly. This bar (33) is the longest in the song and needs a slight *tenuto* on its apex 'dich'.

One sees again the similarity of design to *Ich hab im Traum geweinet* with its dénouement 'Ich wachte auf, und noch immer strömt meine Tränenflut' though Schumann's outburst is more hysterical than Schubert's.

We have taken little heed of the accompaniment thus far and on the face of it, it plays an inconspicuous part going hand in hand with the voice. This is the catch. So many passages have pianoforte and voice moving in unison that keen anticipation on the player's part is necessary; the preservation of perfect unanimity is the accompanist's responsibility and although his playing is at all times shadowy, he himself is very alert. I have heard fine musicians guilty of the following:

and even allowing for my exaggeration it can be understood that the singer in a quandary may ask himself 'With which hand am I supposed to synchronize'?

In bar 7 (Ex. 1) the bass octaves (*pp*) are dark echoes of the voice and must be shaped in the exact same manner. Many of these little interludes lie in a sonorous register

and easily become heavy when they should be hushed.

Only in the postlude does the pianoforte impress itself on the listener's attention for here comes the first *forte* of the entire song. Each chord in 35 (Ex. 4) expresses accumulating bitterness and, in contradiction to the major mode of the singer's last phrase, ends in the deep despairing minor.

X. DAS FISCHERMÄDCHEN

'YOU COMELY fisher-maiden steer your boat to the shore and sit close
to me, we will hold hands and whisper together. Lay your head on my
heart and do not be too afraid, remember you brave the wild sea daily;
my heart like that sea has its storms, its ebb and flow but deep down has
its pearls.'

Hugo Wolf would have thrown the prurient aspect of Heine's words
into prominence, Schubert preferred to play it down, persuaded
perhaps, that the healthy young woman he envisaged was not to be
duped by the addresses of the patronizing young rake from the city
who, far from declaring himself a humble admirer, admits that his heart,
like the sea, is well worth exploring for its hidden treasure.

We can be assured that the girl is not tempted by the wheedling
approach; virtue is unspotted, the boots of the would-be seducer
unwetted and the song is performed without sinister implication.

The *pianissimo* sign—and we know how much Schubert left to the
imagination of the artists—is too frugal to do justice to the picture of
the rocking boat, the constant ups and downs of the vocal line, and
should in my opinion be a *mezzo piano* a mean from which rises and
falls in tone (indicated by me above the stave) can be made without
exaggeration.

An air of complacency flavours the music, noticeable in the introduction, and from the first entry of the voice we are informed that the
philanderer is cocksure his advances will prove irresistible.

Ex.1

The rocking rhythm is always evident in the pianoforte; its block harmony and appearance of solidity are deceiving for it must be made to float lightly. How to achieve this? The secret lies with the 'unimportant' third and sixth beats which are buoyant and are played parenthetically (as becomes a weak beat) with *staccato* touch. *Staccato* yes, but with sustaining pedal so that there is no gap in the tone. The fingers are not under necessity to cling like an organist's to the keys, sensitive pedalling gives them freedom of movement.

Ex. 2

There is a smile in the singer's tone influenced by the lightsome rhythmical flight he heard from his partner.

An enthusiastic rise in bar 10, imitated by the accompaniment, is only natural. 'Komm zu mir und setze dich nieder' is not sung in the same way each time, in 14 it is saucy and *staccato*; in 18, seeing it is embodied in a *crescendo* it is *legato*. Again, 'wir kosen Hand in Hand' is heard thrice, in 21 a little expansion is demanded for the top G flat but 22 is graceful and has its playful 'turn'.

Whether voice and accompaniment are of the same heart and mind is an interesting speculation, they certainly combine in true Schubertian style in their (literally) hand in hand movement in 16 and 20, and again where the *alto* voice moves in contrary motion to the vocal line in 22.

But what of the pianoforte's urgent G flat in 13, its stressed diminished seventh in 17? Perhaps they serve as warnings that the suave salutations from the shore are not so guileless as they sound.

With delightful nonchalance Schubert takes us from the tonic A flat to C flat in the second verse and these premonitions are heard again.

Ex. 3

These misgivings are expressed in the pianoforte part only, the tempter being unaware of them, the singing therefore is care-free.

There are two passages (Ex. 4 and 5) where the vocal line differs slightly from the first verse:

Ex. 4

und fürch-te dich nicht zu sehr; —

In bars 10, 11 (Ex. 1) 'Land' was the high point but in the above the words 'zu sehr' are equal in weight, the quaver not glossed over.

Ex. 5

ver-traust du dich doch sorg — los

Unlike 18, 19 (Ex. 1) where 'nieder' was emphasized, here the high note is made in passing and 'sorglos' made important.

These bars from the final stanza should be contained, if possible in one breath, including the arch in 63, an arch made with seductive grace —and sung quite *piano*; a breath if necessary can be taken after 'Perle'.

Apart from this the third verse is similar to the first. In other words the song ends as it began, and in consequence I like to indulge the fancy that we are back at square one, that the maid is unimpressed by the braggart, that the sea-borne Zerlina sails blithely on, that her Don Giovanni still hopeful, is left high and dry.

XI. DIE STADT

'ON THE distant horizon like a cloud in the gloom I can see the town with its spires. A damp breeze ruffles the grey water while wearily with measured strokes the boatman pulls on his oars. The sun rises once again and its beams reveal only too clearly the place where my beloved was lost to me.'

Misty humidity is marvellously conveyed in this introduction, the blurred outlines in the eerie leaden half-light and the darkness of the water. Even the stirring of air (the first beats of 3, 4, 5) prior to the tired strokes of the rower does not cause a ripple or disturb the mysterious stillness, it portends a breeze that is as yet hardly noticed.

The demisemiquavers in the bass are not to be treated in *tremolando* style as in *Der Atlas*, they are precise but muffled by the sustaining pedal. Like the *pizzicato* on a double-bass the low C's are detached so that the quaver rests are made plain; it would be a mistake to use a *staccato* touch on these notes.

I have never succeeded in playing the *arpeggio* figure as *pianissimo* as I would like; even though the introduction is *una corda* it cannot be too soft. If the player strives to make each note distinct he will be on the wrong tack, these *arpeggi* are blurred as the broken bass octaves were, a wash of sound with a Debussy colour in mind. One pitfall the player seeks to avoid is the signalling of his arrival on the second beat in 3, 4, 5 with a bump; the hand has to jump quickly on to this chord to make it sound as if it belonged to the tremor that preceded it. He listens to himself with care and will not be easily satisfied, being aware that the simplest thing in the world is to make a *sforzando* on the proscribed chord, he strives to prevent this most unwelcome and disturbing splash.

When considering this song the singer, despite the 'Nebelbild' he is describing, should steer a clear course with a definite dynamic pattern in mind.

Ex. 2

Am fer - nen Ho - ri - zon-te er-scheint, wie ein Ne-bel-bild, die
Stadt mit ih-ren Tür-men, in Abenddämmrung ge-hüllt.

The hatred the man feels for the accursed town is not given free rein till the third verse, but in this example we are conscious of an emotion that is held in check. The convulsive nature of the music makes the recommendation 'leise' a misnomer and should not mislead the singer; the thin colour he used in 'ihr Bild' would be unwanted here, the tone in order to unfold and establish the grim scene with meaning must needs be dark. A *piano* is asked for, not a *pianissimo*.

Though the rhythm is convulsive, the score is pointed enough in itself without any exaggeration on the singer's part and it should be treated in strict time.

Breaths can be taken at 8, 10 and 12 but they are not advertized and the singer sings mentally through these rests with relentless concentration. This ukase applies particularly to bar 8.

It will be difficult for his partner if the singer makes his attack on 'Am' (the word beginning on a vowel) without movement of the lips, giving no warning of emission of sound. For the sake of a good ensemble he should give some indication. The *Auftakt* at the start of the third verse gives the pianist all the notice he needs since the first word begins with a consonant.

Even when the vocal line mounts to 'Abenddämmrung gehült' the dark quality should be maintained.

With the second verse we feel the damp penetrating wind whining continuously and ruffling the water as in the introductory bars 3, 4, 5 and above it the voice seems colourless with desolation: 'Alone and palely loitering'.

Ex. 3

Ein feuch-ter Wind - zug kräu -selt die grau -e Was -ser-bahn; mit trau-ri-gem Tak - te ru -dert der Schif -fer in mei-nem Kahn,

Never does the thin sound rise above the level of a *pianissimo* nor should the breaths taken in 19 and 23 be known to anyone save the singer himself.

Stark is the instruction for the final verse and now the volcano erupts, the sight of the place where he last saw his beloved rouses the man to a paroxysm he can no longer hold in check.

Ex.4 stark

Die Son - ne hebt sich noch ein - mal leuchtend vom Bo - den em-
- por, und zeigt mir je -ne Stel-le, wo ich das Lieb-ste ver-lor.

The singer makes this outburst the more telling by having borne it in mind from the song's beginning—first the dark timbre then the white voice and now this.

His triplets in 29 and 33 are weighty with the pianoforte semiquaver making them more ponderous by coming purposefully *after* the third triplet.

Ex. 5

leuchtend vom Bo - ben em -por,   wo ich das Lieb -ste ver-lor.

Obviously 'wo ich das Liebste verlor' is the raison d'être of the composition and must be given dramatic licence, it needs more breadth on the triplets than 29, while 'Liebste' is tremendous in its desperation and is held, though its *tenuto* is not so extravagant as to misshape the phrase. It is advisable for the singer to make no conscious reduction of volume after his top note.

XII. AM MEER

Am Meer like *Ihr Bild*, *Die Stadt* and *Der Doppelgänger* reserves its bitter revelation for the final stanza but from the musical standpoint there is no affinity between them beyond the fact that they are all slow moving. However slow the pace there must be an awareness on the singer's part of motion, he moves forward metaphorically on the ball of the foot not the heel. We postulated in *Die Stadt* that the apogee of the song 'wo ich das Liebste verlor' coming in the last line of the final verse is well considered by the singer before he utters his first note; the broad plan of campaign (not an inflexible one, for modifications of detail qualified by mood—acoustic conditions—and so on are naturally admissible) is clear at the outset and the song is a map in his mind's eye. This applies particularly to such a song as *Am Meer* marked *sehr langsam* and if each individual phrase is given the same forethought the listener will feel the movement, will not lose sight of the pattern. It might be added that the tempo here is *alla breve*.

'The sun's last rays glittered on the wide expanse of sea as we sat silent by a fisherman's lonely hut. Mist arose and the waters swelled, a seagull flew to and fro. Tears came into your loving eyes falling on your white hand and I sank on my knees and kissed them away.

'From that hour my body and spirit are wasted with desire; the unhappy woman's tears have poisoned me.'

Appearances are deceptive; there is much more here than shows on the surface, the singer will unearth deep poignant feeling even without being certain he has the answer to the riddle Heine has posed. Is the

warped silence the outcome of deep misunderstanding or lovers'
jealousy or from some alien cause? There is no way of telling, we only
know that the inarticulate hour is not a blessed one.

The introductory sighs on the pianoforte warn us that all is not well;
the *last* rays of the sun are dejectedly emphasized by the singer, not the
gleaming light on the water.

These long four-bar passages with the accompaniment moving
in sixths under the voice and the tonality of the open key C major combine to evoke an atmosphere of bleakness. Smooth *pianissimo* singing is
needed with hardly a nuance save for the slightest increase up to
'letzten' to allow for a *diminuendo* and a hushed 'scheine'—a word that

tapers away almost to nothing, the quick notes whispered with bated breath like a faint sigh.

They are moments of consequence for they set the mood of the song and need deep thought: the emotion is not to be made obvious though it is there under the surface; the tone though *mezzo voce* is cool and clear.

Ex. 2

The accompaniment's leading note in 11 is made to ring out forlornly as it was in 10. Rising mist and restless sea are painted in the pianoforte whose *demisemiquavers* are not measured out meticulously but resolve into a rapid *tremolo* after a slow start. The *tremolo* can begin *subito* of course though my preference is for a gradual quickening, but in either situation a blurred colour is essential and it cannot be done without sustaining pedal; individual notes must be indistinguishable. Only the *chromatic* and ill-omened descent (12–15) must be prominent and it is made so by accentuating the first bass note in each bar as I have marked in the above example.

'Der Nebel stieg' is *misterioso* and the *crescendo* does not begin until 'das Wasser schwoll' with 'die Möwe' as the apex. At last after returning to *pianissimo* 'Fielen die Tränen' is expressed not by swelling of tone so much as by allowing more time to the stressed notes. This is the first manifestation of deep emotion and is delivered with infinite tenderness.

The second verse is practically identical with the first and the same phrasing obtains, only dynamically should there be a noticeable difference. 'Seit jener Stunde' etc. should have a steeper *crescendo* than that seen in Ex. 2 and a steeper *diminuendo*.

In the singer's last four bars there is a variation:

Ex. 3

Accentuated by the discordant clash in the pianoforte on 'Weib', bars 40 and 41 are really desperate compared with the solicitude of 19, 20.

The final 'Tränen' is as soft and sad as the singer can make it: there is a world of weeping in that bar, it is lingered over with a sorrow that tells of a cause irreparably lost.

Schubert was able to evoke a sultry mood in the C major key when the occasion warranted it; *Meeres Stille* is an instance. Baritones may find the *tessitura* of the original key uncomfortably high and they will hardly be condemned for transposing it one tone down. Unfortunately it will be found that with B flat as its tonic the music will take on a warmer and more soothing quality of sound than is desirable.

Not without reason this has been described as one of Schubert's most difficult songs, for the tone of voice is at once hushed and well-supported; the singer is characterizing a wooer who is unsure of himself yet he sings with absolute control.

XIII. DER DOPPELGÄNGER

'THE NIGHT is still, not a sound in the deserted streets; in this house my beloved one lived. Though she left the town long ago, the house still stands in the same square.

'And there too stands a man who stares upwards and wrings his hands in anguish, I shudder with horror when the moon reveals his face for it is my face, my very self I see.

'You ghostly double, you ghastly fellow, why do you ape the agony of love that tortured me in this same place so many a night in time gone by?'

In its spare disciplined use of line and colour, the matching of music and verse, its immediacy of impact, no song ever written can compare with *Der Doppelgänger*.

Ex.1

The rock on which this composition is built is a repeated eight bar phrase in the pianoforte seen in its entirety from bars 5 to 12; on this *ostinato* persisting for two out of the three stanzas, is carved a pattern so fraught with passion and horror, so demanding of deepest emotion that it leaves the singer spent at the end of it. He always bears in mind that though 'so manche Nacht in alter Zeit' recalls the aching past, he is living and experiencing these emotions in the present; the tragedy is happening to him now.

'Still' and 'Nacht' undoubtedly carry the poetic import of the first vocal phrase as do 'ruhen' and 'Gasse' in the following, but there is an element involved here of which only the performers are aware. It is the exercise of a masterly rhythmical control involving the *unimportant* third beat. For instance 'ist' (5) and the second syllable of 'ruhen' (7) must on no account be hastened; to put it plainly the singer delays his semiquaver in these bars as long as he dares. According to the laws of prosody this is wrong but precedence must be given to musical considerations. This control on the 'weak' beat generates a breathless suspense and is brought into play when the vocal line has the figure ♪ ♪ as in 5, 7, 11 or has a rest as in 8, 10, 12. We shall see how dramatic the effect of this secret prolongation can become as the song proceeds; but it serves another purpose, it is part and parcel of the singer's freedom of declamation for in spite of the sculptured rigidity of the pianoforte the singer's utterance is sometimes quasi-recitative. 'Diesem' (9) for instance loses spirit if adherence to note values is too starched; by reason of its demisemiquavers 'diesem' is a shiver, its short notes paradoxically lose their effect if they are glossed over or hastened, they should be emphasized by deliberation. In reciting the poem you would say '*this* house' not 'this *house*' which is why the phrase curves down to 'Hause' so as not to make it a high point. 'Diesem' is the word that rivets the attention.

Ex.2

It can be seen in these examples how frequently the vocal line is broken up with phrases that look deceptively short, in actuality they are long for the tempo is very slow and the singer must perforce breathe wherever a rest appears but he breathes without any indication he is doing so; his concentration is intense *through* the rests, bars 10, 16, 20, specifically. Such gaps as these would not be countenanced were the words spoken, only in music are they made dramatic and it is the singer's art that makes them significant.

'Auf demselben' is pure recitative and the 'turn' (with no E sharp) is made as slowly as the singer pleases. He exceeds the time limit, there are three beats and a bit more given to bar 21.

A simple expedient for setting the agreed tempo in the introduction is for the pianist to sing mentally the first phrase of the voice part as he plays. With these chords he can exert an influence on his partner by taking especial care that his fourth chord is no whit shorter than the others. He should resist the impulse to make an increase of tone as he rises to the third bar, there is no necessity for it—all is *pianissimo*, the night is still.

Schubert's phrase lines are only in evidence in the first verse and are not seen again until the postlude, but while there they should be heeded; thus bars 4 and 5 are not joined, a minute comma can be made between them as I have marked and this anticipates that very slight suspension on the third beat in the voice part we have been at pains to discuss.

The pianoforte treble in 13 echoes forlornly 'wohnte mein Schatz' and again gives the shiver of bar 9. (Its dying fall recalls 'im letzten Abendscheine' of *Am Meer.*) These demisemiquavers are quicker and if possible quieter than the singer's and are only executed after practice and careful listening. They are the echo of a sigh; the fingers are actually in light contact with those three notes before they are depressed —they are not struck, they are brushed—heard ever so faintly: this applies to 23 as well.

But bar 25 is another proposition. It is a warning. For on that first chord there is a sharpness of touch, a nervous start, like a quick turn of the head, as the ghostly figure catches the eye. It is still *pianissimo* but the pianist feels the difference *inside* him as he plays. This electricity is conveyed to the singer who now embarks on the first of three great climbing phrases, all starting with a menacing *piano*, all culminating in a frightening *fortississimo*.

Again the drawn out third beat comes into play. Both artists despite their inner excitement must resist the temptation to accelerate. This is particularly trying for the singer: at 27, 29, 31 he thinks his partner will never bring himself to strike the first chord of these bars and without this beat he cannot move, moreover 'Mensch und starrt'—'Hände vor Schmerzensgewalt' are—like the passage of 10, 11—joined together in *thought*. The more the rest is protracted the harder for the singer but he must face up to it like a man.

A suspicion of a *portamento* on 'starrt' is desirable for it helps us feel the growth of the *crescendo*. 'Ringt' has agonizingly clear enunciation again deserving of breadth, while 'Schmerzensgewalt' is tremendous and prolonged; the last two syllables are bitten out and should not be given a conscious *diminuendo*, the octave drop of the voice gives them less volume without the singer contributing to it.

der Mond zeigt mir   mei-ne   eig - ne Ge - stalt. ___

With the same pianoforte ground the singer launches himself on the second of his climbs. By comparing 35 with 26 it can now be seen how simply but realistically the shudder is portrayed. Heine did not choose a pleasant sounding word to suit this contingency, 'graust' is no more euphonius than the English equivalent and the singer should make no effort to beautify its onomatopoeia. Time must be allowed for the grinding consonants G—R—R and the pianist is prepared for this.

Schubert again varies the vocal line (compare phrase 38 to 41 with 29 to 32) as we are hoisted to the song's zenith: 'zeigt' is a long quaver but 'meine eigne Gestalt' (unhurried quavers in 40) is terrific and needs all the power possible. The passage has led up to the highest note in the vocal line; this is as it should be, but I look on it as the tonal climax not only for the top note's sake but because it is the instant of fearful revelation—half expected and dreaded. Horror is not to be short lived, the top G is held beyond its written length and released just before the third beat of 42. Only the pianoforte makes a *diminuendo*, not the singer who keeps to a relentless *fortississimo* and violently ejects the final consonants. (It should be borne in mind by the singer that though a *fortississimo* is demanded at 'Schmerzensgewald' Ex. 3, he would do well to save an extra ounce of strength for 'meine eigne Gestalt' if it is at all possible. Only experience and generalship will allow him to deploy these hidden reserves without the listener knowing they were there.)

There has been no relaxation up to this point from the iron control of pace the artists have exercised and they are to be admired for maintaining it. But now for the first time comes an *accelerando* whose effect is immeasurably heightened through not having been used—or rather wasted—before.

With conspicuous genius Schubert, with the arrival of the *accelerando* abandons the *ostinato* accompaniment and in its stead gives us a chromatic ascent up to 'äffst' with its afflictive D sharp minor chord. To sneer at one's self is odious and it is so typical a Heine stroke that much must be made of it; in fact the momentum is stayed to give vent to the gall the word 'äffst' inspires. 'Was äffst du nach mein Liebesleid' sees the end of the *accelerando*: the situation is too fearful, the man too close to collapse for any idea of hurry to be entertained. (In truth there is no indication where the composer intended *tempo primo* to be resumed; surely an oversight since to continue gathering speed up to the song's end would be inconceivable.) Above all 49 must not be hurried—this passage 'tortured me in this same place' is to be laboured and suffered over, further, it is a stepping-stone to the heart-rending 'so manche Nacht in alter Zeit' which I feel is the song's emotional moment of truth. The stricken man could say no more after the tear-choked retrospect of these soul searing bars. What more is there to add to this collapse, to this self-condemnation of a lifetime wasted in hopeless love?

'Meine eigne Gestalt' asked for full power to the very end of its explosive consonant and, as I said is the dynamic apex but it does not put such a pressure on the singer's resources as the final passage. It is one thing to sing *fortississimo*, it is another to let us hear this full-throated tone dwindle and weaken to a *pianissimo*. The *diminuendo*, as in the accompaniment, is felt while the F sharp is being held but the note is given a *fermata* thus giving space before the *diminuendo* takes over.

I used the term 'tear-choked' but if the voice were literally choked no sound would be heard; only the singer's technical mastery and complete absorption in the drama will do justice to this imperishable music.

The *ostinato* is resumed at the beginning of the postlude

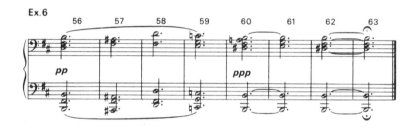

but at 59 we hear surprisingly the chord of C major whose ghostly impact is like a shiver. These chords are as shadowy as ever. It is uncanny how the final cadence though in the major mode does not bring the slightest easement; hushed it is but it cannot quiet the fever and pain.

How discerning Wilhelm Müller was to bring his *Winterreise* to a close with *Der Leiermann*. *Der Doppelgänger* should also be the end. Were I a singer with the fourteen songs of 'Schwanengesang' on my programme I would leave the stage after it out of respect for it, returning to my audience after they had had time to recover and I had regained my poise before performing *Die Taubenpost*. The latter is a lovable little creation but not to be appreciated while the metaphysical over-tones of *Der Doppelgänger* are still echoing in our minds.

XIV. DIE TAUBENPOST

By VIRTUE of its inclusion in the *Schwanengesang*, *Die Taubenpost* is the best known of the settings of Johann Gabriel Seidl and like his *Wiegenlied* ('Wie sich der Äuglein') has that guileless air to which Schubert's tender humanity was quick to respond. Both songs, the lullaby particularly, are somewhat generous in proportion to their subject matter but *Die Taubenpost* is so haunting, so blissfully innocent that one's heart is warmed by it.

The carrier pigeon, tireless, takes all the love messages to the precious one's dwelling. By day or by night he flies with them and faithfully returns with an answer. And what is this dear messenger's name? He is called *Die Sehnsucht*—Love's Yearning.

Syncopation is a fascinating feature of the accompaniment and is absent only in one or two of the interludes or when the pianoforte is piping high up in the air.

A happy balance between left hand and right is to be sought. The importance of the first beat in each bar is shewn in this introduction, it defines the syncopation which would not exist without it. But in making this definition the left hand does not become earthbound; that first

Ex.1

beat in each group of four quavers is always *staccato*—light and airy—
as marked, with the following three quavers *legato*.

The treble is another story; the chords here in each bar's second half
are gently detached, with a touch not a bit like that used for the bass
staccato. This figure (the first four bars) is repeated often and it sings
with quiet serenity.

It is gratifying to hear a smiling quality of tone from the singer after
the traumatic experience of the Heine songs, and he revels in a smooth
stream of sound in contrast to the accompaniment's *staccato* fluttering.
Later in the song he will have reason to wax enthusiastic but in the first
two stanzas (up to bar 25) he should avoid loading these simple sentiments with exaggerated expression or conventional nuances.

The momentary modulation to B major in the tiny interlude is to
be relished

especially the little caper at 14 where the semiquaver is not to be snapped
on to the A sharp but sung with affection. I use the verb 'sung' intentionally. The *legato* signs are there with intent as they are in 26 to
29, another warm interlude.

Again this is to be sung. The *legato* in 27 is well contrasted with
the detached chords in the preceding bar. My marks above the stave
in 28 suggest the slightest hesitation, not enough to disturb but to give
more grace to the forward progression: if 28 is played in strict time it
can easily become matter of fact.

A temptation to be resisted is to make a *crescendo* with two rising passages at 30 to 33 and 34 to 37

for the instruction is *pianissimo* and remains so for 'heimlich hinein'. The turn on 'heimlich' is taken in the singer's stride without fuss; it is contrived delicately and comes at the end of 30—before the bar line—robbing the last syllable of 'Fenster'.

The tears in the B flat section are not really impassioned,

si - cher nicht, gar eif - rig dient sie mir, gar

eif - rig dient sie mir.

in fact the *crescendo* (the singer's first) starting with a *pianissimo* is only expanded, vide Schubert, up to a *piano*. This is a little too reticent and I suggest *mezzo piano* be allowed, but no more; the singer because of his top notes does not become a Heldentenor. The texture of the writing cannot suffer rude treatment and if too much voice is used the pianoforte will not be heard with its syncopations and pipings which must of necessity be light and graceful. It is a trap for the singer and if he lacks sensitivity he falls into it: here is another

Ex.6

die Taub ist so mir treu!

'Taub' obviously deserves more emphasis than 'die'; anybody can do it the other way round.

    It is now we reach the salient point of the song with the passage 'He is called Love's Yearning—did you know it?' and Schubert paves the way by a climbing and loudening phrase in C major to be followed immediately by an entrancing fall into A major.

More volume is wanted at 74 (and again at 89 where the words are repeated in E flat) than anywhere else and its effect is to make the ensuing *pianissimo* all the more melting.

This page of music clutches the heart if it is sung beautifully. It is all *molto legato* and begs for affection from the singer, a feeling for it inducing him to dwell on 'sie heisst' (76, 77) with tenderness and to sing it so very softly. He who hurries slickly—in strict time-off 'sie' not only lacks discrimination but makes it obvious that he does not care a damn.

Die Taubenpost has a magic that is Schubert's very own. How typical of the man after his mighty Goethe songs, his transfiguration of Wilhelm Müller's verses, his new vision with Heine that his last song should be unpretentious. He arrived quietly on to the scene and he left it quietly. 'There was a world of things left for him to do', wrote Capell, 'he can be imagined in the 1830's engaged with Eichendorff, Uhland, Mörike, and going deeper into Rückert and Heine. But the time was refused him'.

INDEX

(Excluding references to Franz Schubert himself. For the 58 songs comprising the three cycles, see list of Contents pages vii and viii.)